"Dad, look at this saddle we found in the catalog!"

Darci broke off the kiss as abruptly as Jordan did, her eyes snapping open to see his daughter standing in front of them on the deck with her friend Jenny, holding a Western tack catalog. Both girls stared wide-eyed at them, Michaela's gaze accusing.

"How could you kiss her?" Michaela shrieked. Then she turned and fled down the steps below deck.

The look she'd given Darci could have melted the anchor and left them all to drift away across the reservoir. Darci was pretty sure Michaela would have run much farther than below deck if there had been anywhere else for her to go. Jenny looked embarrassed as she trailed after her.

"Oh, God," Darci said. "Jordan, I'm so sorry."

"I'm the one who kissed you," he said, then headed after his daughter.

D1409044

Dear Reader,

My dad taught me there is a reason for everything. I had a hard time believing that when he very suddenly passed away while I was writing this book. It took me many months to even begin to get back on my feet. But as clichéd as it may sound, my father's death made me see life from a different angle.

I began to remember how he'd taught me not to ever say "goodbye," only "so long for now." This is a belief of our people—the Cherokees—and something I began to take comfort in. I know I'll see my dad again, and I know his death, as devastating as it was, is a turning point for me.

I realized that my heroine in *Ranch at River's End* had reached a turning point in her life as well. When Darci Taylor's son scares a cafeteria full of students half out of their minds, Darci decides they need a fresh start in the small mountain town of River's End.

But things don't go as smoothly as Darci hoped with the transition to her new world. Jordan Drake is an emergency room physician whose own life was turned upside down two years earlier when his wife was killed and his daughter wounded. He's protective of Michaela, and when Jordan finds out Darci and her son have moved in four houses down from his own, he isn't at all happy.

I had a great time taking my hero and heroine down the path they had to travel, and in watching how they dealt with their individual issues and—most important of all—how they dealt with their growing attraction to one another. And trust me, they went kicking and screaming!

I love hearing from my readers. You can reach me at BrendaMott@hotmail.com. Please reference the book title on the subject line.

My best to you!

Brenda Mott

Ranch at River's End
Brenda Mott

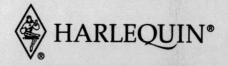

TORONTO • NEW YORK • LONDON
AMSTERDAM • PARIS • SYDNEY • HAMBURG
STOCKHOLM • ATHENS • TOKYO • MILAN • MADRID
PRAGUE • WARSAW • BUDAPEST • AUCKLAND

Recycling programs
for this product may
not exist in your area.

ISBN-13: 978-0-373-78399-1

RANCH AT RIVER'S END

Copyright © 2010 by Brenda Mott.

All rights reserved. Except for use in any review, the reproduction or utilization of this work in whole or in part in any form by any electronic, mechanical or other means, now known or hereafter invented, including xerography, photocopying and recording, or in any information storage or retrieval system, is forbidden without the written permission of the publisher, Harlequin Enterprises Limited, 225 Duncan Mill Road, Don Mills, Ontario, Canada M3B 3K9.

This is a work of fiction. Names, characters, places and incidents are either the product of the author's imagination or are used fictitiously, and any resemblance to actual persons, living or dead, business establishments, events or locales is entirely coincidental.

This edition published by arrangement with Harlequin Books S.A.

For questions and comments about the quality of this book please contact us at Customer_eCare@Harlequin.ca.

® and TM are trademarks of the publisher. Trademarks indicated with ® are registered in the United States Patent and Trademark Office, the Canadian Trade Marks Office and in other countries.

www.eHarlequin.com

Printed in U.S.A.

ABOUT THE AUTHOR

When Brenda Mott isn't busy writing or rescuing animals—she has more than thirty dogs at any given time—she enjoys curling up with a good book (naturally!), or taking in the beauty of Tennessee's Powell River on horseback, or on foot with a few of her dogs. Brenda can trace her family roots back to the Cherokees who walked the Trail of Tears, and her ranch—twenty-one acres deep in the Tennessee woods—is located on part of what used to be the original claims of the Cherokee Nation.

Brenda's stories most often have a theme of strong family ties and values. They also reflect her love of horses—and of her home state of Colorado—by having a ranch-themed plot. Her works have won several awards including Best Series Romance from *RT Book Reviews,* but her greatest reward comes in entertaining her readers. She enjoys writing romance most of all, because there's always a guaranteed happy ending. She loves hearing from her readers. Reach her at BrendaMott@hotmail.com.

Books by Brenda Mott

HARLEQUIN SUPERROMANCE

1037—SARAH'S LEGACY
1127—COWGIRL, SAY YES
1211—THE NEW BABY
1257—THE CHOSEN CHILD
1286—TO PROTECT HIS OWN
1369—MAN FROM MONTANA
1430—THE SHERIFF OF SAGE BEND
1526—COWBOY FOR KEEPS

This book is dedicated in loving memory
of my phenomenal dad.
I miss you more than even a writer's words
can say.
Ah-nah-gee-sss-dee nahs-squah
Oo-ney-tlah-nuh-he.
(Go with God.)

CHAPTER ONE

JORDAN DRAKE WATCHED his daughter moving quickly up the sidewalk to school despite the cane she relied on. Hard to believe Michaela was already in the seventh grade. A now-familiar sadness threatened to overwhelm him. Sandra should be here, sharing this significant milestone in their daughter's life with him. But this was no time for regrets—Sandra wouldn't have wanted that. He had to keep moving forward.

The quiet drive to the hospital always calmed him, and he glanced up now at the rough-hewn mountain peaks, scattered with scrub oak, juniper and sagebrush, that surrounded River's End.

The rural town was plunked down in the middle of some of the prettiest country western Colorado had to offer. With a small population, it was, Jordan had always believed, a good place to raise a child.

But tragedy had found him even here.

Shaking off the thought, he focused on the sun-filled, late-August day. He was sorry he couldn't be outdoors, but he loved his job. Being an E.R. physician at River's End Regional Hospital had its perks. Working three days on, three days off gave him plenty of time to spend with Michaela.

After parking his black Ford Explorer in his designated spot, Jordan headed inside. He'd barely scanned the reports when a patient—a boy Jordan knew to be the best fullback on their high school team—was rushed into the E.R. with a head wound. Typically, it was bleeding profusely.

"His brother hit him with a machete," said the trembling woman hovering over Bruce Wilkins.

"It wasn't a machete, Mom, it was a big knife." The husky kid sighed in exasperation. "And it was an accident. I'm fine." He grinned as Jordan pressed a wad of gauze against the wound with gloved hands. "But I don't know about that lady at the check-in desk. She passed out cold when she saw this." Bruce pointed at his wound.

Shirley? Had to be, Jordan thought. She was the one who usually handled the front desk. But he was surprised to hear she'd fainted. Shirley had worked at the hospital for years and seen all kinds of injuries.

"She did?" *Go figure.*

"Yep. And she hit her head, too, so you might

be puttin' stitches in both of us, Doc. I can wait if you need to stitch her up first."

"You cannot wait!" Donna Wilkins scolded her son. "I'm sure Dr. Drake isn't the only doctor here in the E.R."

"Actually, I am the only physician on hand at the moment, but Dr. Samuels is just finishing his shift. We'll page him if we need to."

Jordan's professional calm hid his concern. Someone needed to see if Shirley was okay.

He was about to duck out quickly to check on the receptionist when a wheelchair rolled into the adjoining exam room, which was partitioned off by a curtain. Jordan couldn't see the patient, but he heard her protests over the squeak of the chair's rubber wheels.

"This is ridiculous. I'm fine, really."

Not Shirley.

"We'll let Dr. Drake be the judge of that," Molly Parker said. She'd been a nurse at River's End Regional for as long as Jordan could remember. "Now get yourself up there on that exam table, Missy, and I'll see where the doc's at."

If any more people came into the E.R., he'd definitely have to have Dr. Samuels paged.

"I'm here," Jordan said. He parted the curtain enough to look discreetly through the opening.

A petite woman with short, blond hair was in the process of exiting the wheelchair.

"Is Shirley all right?" Jordan asked. "We'll need to page Dr. Samuels, Molly, to check on her."

The nurse gave him a strange look. "Shirley's fine—why?"

"I don't need a doctor at all," the blond woman protested as she reluctantly climbed onto the exam table under Molly's watchful eye. Gingerly, she touched the goose egg Jordan spotted on her forehead. "It's just a bump."

"You hit the corner of the desk and lost consciousness," Molly said firmly. "*But* I think you can wait while the doctor stitches Bruce up, right, Dr. Drake? Or do you want me to page Dr. Samuels?" She looked as confused as Jordan felt.

He frowned. "I thought it was Shirley who hit her head."

"No, no," Molly said, her mop of dark curls bobbing as she shook her own head. "Dr. Drake, meet Darci Taylor, our new receptionist. Shirley's training her to replace Tiffany."

Who had gone into early labor yesterday afternoon. Now everything fell into place.

"Jordan Drake," he said. "You must be from the temp service." He held out his hand and the woman placed hers in it. She had a soft palm, but a surprisingly strong grip, and the bluest eyes he'd ever seen. The scent of vanilla perfume wafted his way, subtle and pleasant.

"That's right," she said. "Nice to meet you. Are you any relation to Dr. Nina Drake?"

"She's my sister." The psychologist of the family. He wondered how Darci Taylor knew Nina. Was she a patient?

Making a quick assessment of her head injury, Jordan nodded. "This can wait a few moments if you don't mind."

"Not at all. Please—take care of that young man." She gestured toward the curtained partition, looking pale again.

"I'll be with you as soon as I can, Darci." Her name rolled over his tongue like candy. She was suntanned and pretty—her petite figure all curves beneath the floral-print skirt and silky T-shirt she wore. How on earth had he missed her?

Whoa. What was wrong with him? He saw female patients every day, many of them as pretty or prettier than Darci Taylor.

But none with eyes that blue.

DARCI FELT LIKE A COMPLETE idiot. Her first day—Lord, her first few minutes—on the job, and she'd fainted like some Victorian lady. When she'd accepted the position at the hospital through the temp agency, she'd somehow never connected working at a reception desk with seeing blood. *Duh*.

This *was* the emergency department, and she'd better get her act together in a happy hurry if she intended to keep the position. Her part-time job giving riding lessons on her aunt and uncle's ranch wasn't nearly enough to pay the bills.

Being a single mother wasn't easy, and this last year had been hell, but she'd managed to get through it.

Darci shifted farther back on the exam table, waiting her turn. It was impossible not to eavesdrop on Dr. Jordan Drake in the adjoining area. His deep voice was calm and patient as he tended to the boy who'd been brought in with the head wound. And then he laughed at something Bruce Wilkins said, and tiny goose bumps danced along her arms and neck.

The man had seemed so serious—she wondered what it took to make Dr. Cowboy Boots laugh.

Now where had that thought come from? Through a slit in the adjoining curtain, she couldn't help but steal a peek at the doctor. He didn't look much older than her own thirty-four—and met the old cliché standard of tall, dark and handsome.

But what sort of doctor wore jeans and cowboy

boots with his scrub top? He looked more like a veterinarian who specialized in large animals. Well…River's End was a tiny ranching community. Maybe the guy treated both humans and livestock.

Darci's head throbbed, the bump feeling more like a cantaloupe than a goose egg. But she couldn't afford to take any time off work.

She'd combined two part-time jobs in North-glenn, outside of Denver, before moving here with Chris. Working for a temp service, and the twenty-plus hours a week she'd put in at a local stable afforded her the means to take care of her thirteen-year-old son and she hoped to do the same thing in River's End.

She planned to work extra hard for Aunt Stella and Uncle Leon. They were the only people who hadn't turned their backs on her and Chris when her son had committed a crime most people weren't willing to look past.

Shaking off the black thoughts, Darci let her mind drift back to handsome Dr. Drake. She couldn't resist sneaking another peek through the curtain at those Western boots and jeans he wore. Professional though he was, he still looked pretty hot in them. Definitely cowboy casual.

The only thing that ruined his cowboy image, was his smooth hands. It had felt so good when she'd shaken hands with him.

His hair, straight and thick and dark as his espresso eyes, was just long enough to brush the top of his collar. Her fingers itched to touch it.

What was wrong with her? Darci gave herself a mental kick, remembering that she had more serious things to take care of in her life right now. She didn't have time for good-looking doctors.

Dr. Cowboy Boots? the imp in the back of her mind teased.

Not even him, Darci thought, wondering if the bump on her head had affected her thinking. Still, she tried to imagine what Jordan's face had looked like just now when he laughed. But all she could picture were those dark eyes.

The curtain parted and Darci nearly yelped.

"So you've got quite the bump there," Jordan said as he moved toward her, chart in hand.

His professional voice was gentle, caring, and yet oh, so sexy.

"I—I skipped breakfast and felt a little dizzy," she said, unwilling to admit she'd flat-out fainted. She could have eaten the Grand Slam breakfast at the local Denny's and she still would've passed out at the sight of Bruce Wilkins's gaping head wound.

"Mmm-hmm." Jordan laid down the clipboard, lathered his hands to the elbows at the nearby sink, then snapped on a fresh pair of gloves before stepping up beside her.

Was he going to touch her?

Of course he was. He was a doctor after all. He could hardly examine her head from across the room. But right now Darci could use a little distance between them. The antiseptic smell of the hospital was overpowered by Jordan's own clean scent. Soap, pure male and...what else? Words like *woodsy* and *musky* came to mind, but that wasn't right either. Jordan didn't strike her as the musky type.

No. His scent was more like fresh squeezed limes and—

Tequila, the imp prompted, inspiring images of body shots and salt and...good grief, she'd hit her head all right! And lost her mind in the process.

Jordan frowned in concentration and gently touched the lump on her forehead.

"Tender?" he asked.

Darci winced. "Very."

She felt raw and vulnerable sitting there with his wonderful, strong and capable hands on her...and aching for more.

It had been way too long since she'd enjoyed a man's touch, or even a simple date for that matter. The threats Christopher had made at his former school in Northglenn had taken over their lives, consumed Darci day and night for the past several months.

"Looks like you could use a couple of stitches," Jordan said, jarring her from her thoughts. "Or maybe we can put some butterfly clamps on the laceration. Less scarring that way."

"Sounds good," Darci said. She tried not to flinch as he tended to her wound.

"There, that should do it. Don't get it wet for a few days, and let me know if you notice any heat or further swelling. If the pain gets bad, take some Tylenol."

"What—not two aspirin and call you in the morning?" Darci blamed her head injury on the lame quip. Just because he'd eyeballed her a little when she'd first come in...or had he? Maybe she'd imagined it. But it didn't matter anyway. Just didn't mean a thing. For all she knew there was a Mrs. Cowboy Boots in the picture.

So why couldn't she quiet that damned imp in her head?

Jordan studied her as he peeled off his gloves, then reached for a pen and notepad. He scribbled something, and Darci spoke quickly. "I don't need a prescription. It doesn't hurt that bad."

He handed over the scrap of paper and Darci looked at it and nearly choked. He'd jotted down a pair of phone numbers in a neat, looping scrawl unlike the stereotypical hard-to-read doctor's handwriting.

"Call me if you have any complications— excessive headache, vomiting, that sort of thing," he said. "Either Dr. Samuels or I will be on call."

"Thanks." Darci folded the slip of paper and put it in her purse.

She could've looked up the hospital number in the phone book. Had he given her his home number?

Don't be silly.

Maybe she could ask him to write out a prescription for her after all. One for a woman who'd been too long without a date. An anti-man drug. Maybe an anti*his*tamine. Inwardly she snickered at her own lame humor.

Lord, she'd had no idea a head injury could turn her into a ditz.

Call me?

Jordan put his key in the front-door lock and opened the dead bolt. What had he been thinking? There was no reason to have given Darci Taylor his home phone number in addition to the one at the hospital. At least it wasn't his cell. He didn't need to be bothered day and night with minor medical emergencies.

But then, she probably wasn't the type to do

that anyway. Darci seemed like a strong, confident woman who took matters into her own hands.

You want her to call.

The voice inside his head taunted him as he deactivated the alarm and called out to Michaela that he was home.

Darci had looked vulnerable as she sat in the exam room with a head injury, though. She obviously wasn't cut out to work in the E.R. admittance. Maybe she'd get a job elsewhere and then he could stop thinking about her.

Besides—he hadn't been interested in a woman since Sandra had died. No point in starting now.

"Mac!" he called again, using the nickname his daughter preferred.

"In the kitchen, Dad."

She was at the table, eating a frozen yogurt and working on her laptop. The way her head was tilted, with her long, light brown hair caught up in a ponytail, she looked so much like her mother.

Jordan's chest tightened.

"Is that homework?" She was allowed online, but with limited access.

He had to protect his daughter.

Michaela nodded. "I'm writing a report on the opening chapter of a book we're reading." She rolled her eyes. "Why do teachers always make us read boring things instead of something we'd actually like?"

"Good question." He bent and kissed the top of her head. "One that kids asked even in my generation."

"They had books back then?"

"Very funny. What's this?" He picked up a piece of paper from the countertop. A flyer about parent-teacher meetings and an open house being held at the school a week from Tuesday.

"It's a welcome-to-the-school-year thing," Michaela said. "Sorta lame, but I guess we're supposed to go."

"They're serving refreshments," he said. "At least we can score some cookies."

Michaela returned his grin. "You'll like my homeroom teacher. She's cool."

"Awesome. Can't wait. How about we go out on the boat this weekend?"

"Cool! Can Jenny come? We want to check out some new horse magazines."

The cabin cruiser slept four, and Michaela's best friend often came along on overnight excursions as well as day trips.

"We'll see. Right now, why don't you just worry about what you want on your pizza."

"We're going to Trail Inn?"

Restaurants in River's End were a scarce

commodity, but Trail Inn was the best pizza joint within fifty miles, and his daughter's favorite. "You'd better know it," Jordan said. "As soon as I change out of my scrubs."

"And after I check on Chewy again." The stray dog Mac had begged him to take in that summer had come with a surprise—puppies, born a week ago.

The medium-sized, red-and-white dog had turned out to be a blessing. Caring for Chewy and her puppies had been the best form of therapy for Michaela—something that made his little girl smile more than she had since her mother's death. And Chewy was a good watchdog—something he'd wanted to get Mac, though he'd been a little leery of the more aggressive breeds.

Chewy had quickly become a spoiled family member, temporarily distracting Mac from her obsession with horses. She'd been trying to talk Jordan into buying her a horse like her friend Jenny's, which Michaela wanted to ride. Her hip injury would likely never get much better, and Jordan was worried that a fall from a horse might make it worse.

"I'll run next door and say thanks to Louise." The neighbor kept an eye out for Michaela, even kept his daughter at her house at times, when Jordan wasn't home. "Then we're off. We can swing by and rent a couple of DVDs—heck, it's Friday night. I'll even watch *The Sisterhood of the Traveling Trousers* again."

Friday nights had always been pizza and movie night for Mac and Sandra.

"Da-ad." His daughter snickered. "It's Traveling *Pants,* and there's a part two, you know."

"No, I didn't know. Hey—even better. We can watch both of them."

"I know what you're trying to do," she said, quirking her mouth into a crooked little pucker—a Sandra habit. "And I love you for it, Dad. Thanks." But her eyes held sadness.

"I love you, too, snicker-doodle."

As soon as Jordan Drake had finished tending to her injury, Darci had insisted on going right back to work, but Shirley demanded she take it easy. "You just watch me work, and you'll get the hang of things," the older woman said. "We'll worry about the details when you're feeling better."

Things had been fairly slow for the rest of the morning, though they picked up in the afternoon. By the time four-thirty rolled around, Darci was ready to go home. She was tired, her head was throbbing, and she was worried about Christopher. She'd asked Stella to keep an eye on him at the ranch after school until she could make other arrangements, and Chris had been furious.

"I don't need a babysitter," he'd said. "I'm old enough to stay home alone for a couple of hours."

"Yes, you are," Darci had told him. "But age and privilege are two different things, and you're going to have to earn my trust before I leave you by yourself."

"Whatever. Just do me a favor, and don't ask old lady Bataway to watch me."

Their neighbor, Eileen Hathaway, was a busy-body and overprotective of her enormous dog, a Newfoundland.

"Disrespect isn't going to help you any. And I'm sure there's not enough money in the bank to get Mrs. Hathaway to babysit you anyway."

Now as she drove toward the Shadow S Ranch in a wind-blown sprinkling of rain, she hoped Christopher hadn't given Aunt Stella a hard time. Of course, if he had, Stella would likely put a boot to his butt. Maybe that was what he needed. Maybe she'd been so busy worrying over everything that had happened in Northglenn that she hadn't been hard enough on him.

Lord knows she'd experienced her share of anger and frustration. Yet she'd made a huge effort to tamp her feelings down and cave in to

Christopher's wants and needs. No more, though. She was through being Mommy Doormat.

Maybe Nina Drake could give her some helpful guidance when she saw Christopher on Thursday. Darci had requested a few minutes of the appointment time for her and Dr. Drake to talk.

At the ranch house, Darci rapped on the front door, then pushed it open, glad to get out of the wet weather. Immediately she was treated to the smell of home cooking. Stella and Leon's dog—a big cream-colored mutt of undetermined heritage—greeted her with wagging tail. "Hey, Jake." She scratched the dog behind his ears. In the kitchen, she found Stella at the stove, Chris and Leon nowhere in sight.

"Hi, Aunt Stella. Where's Chris?"

"Doing his homework in the den. How was your first day?" Then she noticed the butterfly clamps and frowned, taking hold of Darci and steering her toward the window, where she could see the wound better. "Lands sakes, what happened to you?"

Darci shrugged sheepishly. "I fainted. It's no big deal. I'm fine."

"Fainted? What happened? Here, sit down and put your feet up. Want something to drink?"

"Aunt Stella, I'm fine, really." But Darci obliged her aunt, kicking off her heels and propping her feet on a kitchen chair. She twisted the cap off the Diet Coke Stella set in front of her and took a long swig.

Her aunt demanded all the details, and Darci was halfway through her story when Christopher came out of the den and headed for the fridge.

She turned to face her thirteen-year-old son, who was nearly as tall as she was. He needed a haircut. His shaggy brown mop, the ends dyed black, hung in his eyes. Green eyes like his father's. The man who'd left them a year ago without looking back.

"Pull up your jeans," Darci said. Normally, she would've let Chris's sagging pants hang beneath his boxers without comment. *Pick your battles, Darci.* Their former counselor's advice. But today she was in no mood to be conciliatory.

"They won't stay anyway."

"That's what your belt is for."

He grinned. "You actually fainted at work? Bet that went over big—passing out in the E.R."

"Hey, it's not funny." Then Darci softened. "Okay, maybe a little. I was pretty embarrassed." Especially when she'd had to undergo Jordan's ministrations.

"Don't eat too much," Stella scolded as Chris

rummaged around for a snack. "I've got a pot of chili cooking."

"You didn't have to cook for us," Darci said.

"No big deal, kid. I figured you'd be tuckered, and Leon went to a lodge meeting so it was just gonna be me and a TV dinner. Now I'm doubly glad I threw something together, seeing as how you're the walking wounded." She nudged her niece's knee affectionately as she passed by the chair where Darci had propped her legs.

"I *love* your chili, so I'm not going to protest too much," Darci said. Stella used three kinds of beans, plus lots of chopped celery, onions and garlic.

Chris turned from the fridge with an apple and a wedge of cheese. "Save some of that for the chili." She indicated the cheddar. "You getting your homework done?"

He wrinkled his nose as he sliced off a chunk of cheese on the cutting board Stella had been using. "We have to write a report for environmental studies on how we can be green at school. I'm about three pages short of the required four."

"I'm sure you'll come up with something," Darci said, glad to see he was actually settling back into public school after homeschooling for the final semester of last year. "Do you like your teachers so far?"

He shrugged. "They're okay. Oh, yeah, that reminds me." Stuffing the cheese into his mouth, he dragged his backpack off a chair. "There's a parent-teacher thing coming up." He rummaged in his pack and handed her the flyer. "Do we have to go?"

"Well, if it's parent-teacher, I don't see why you should have to…oh, wait," Darci said. "They're having an open house. And the skate park behind the school will be open, too. Says there'll be plenty of adult supervision. You should go, Chris. It'll be fun."

"Oh, Mom." He slumped as if she'd shot him with a poison dart. "I don't need to go to the skate park with a bunch of teacher's aides watching my every move."

"Come on, Christopher," Stella said. "Listen to your mom. If you don't want to take your skateboard, at least you can see what the school looks like at night…show your mom your locker, visit with your friends."

"Trust me," he said, "I don't have any friends."

"Well, then this will be a good way to make some." Stella stirred the pot of chili. "I always thought it was fun to be at school at nighttime."

"You're going," Darci said, remembering her earlier resolve to stop coddling him.

"Fine. I'll be in the den doing my slave work if anyone needs me."

Stella chuckled once he'd gone. "Kids. They make everything so dramatic."

Then she sobered, as if remembering just how dramatic things had gotten back at North Star Middle School in Northglenn.

CHAPTER TWO

DARCI THANKED AUNT STELLA for the chili, and for watching Chris, then hurried out to the car after him. It had begun to rain harder now, quarter-sized drops pattering down in cold splashes against her skin as she rushed toward her red Chevy Cavalier.

Christopher sat in the front seat, listening to his iPod. It was one of the privileges he'd recently earned back for good behavior. Darci shoved the container of leftovers Aunt Stella had sent with them into his lap before sliding behind the wheel. The windshield wipers swished out a steady rhythm as she drove, making her way down the county road and on through town. She hadn't gone more than the few blocks that made up the downtown area, when she spotted a familiar figure at the side of the road.

Jordan Drake stood next to a black Ford Explorer, examining a flat rear tire.

Oh, dear. Should she stop? Or did he have things under control?

Darci glanced in her rearview mirror and saw

him kick the flat in frustration, then head back toward the driver's door. No spare? She supposed he could walk to the gas station, but it wasn't in her to ignore someone in need of help, and besides, who wanted to walk in the rain?

Beside her, Christopher paid no attention to the fact that Darci had slowed the car. His head nodded to the beat of what was likely Southern-country-rock—his favorite. She turned into the parking lot of a church, flipped a U-turn and headed back out onto Main Street.

Christopher frowned, pulling off one earbud. "Hey, where are you going, Mom?"

"To help someone," she said.

"Huh?" He yanked out the other earbud. "But I want to get home and watch TV." His favorite reality show was coming on, another privilege he'd regained.

"Chris, we can't leave someone stranded at the side of the road."

"But you're always telling me it's not smart to stop for strangers."

"He's not a stranger. I work with him—well, sort of." She wrinkled her nose, remembering the way Jordan's hands had felt as he'd tended to her head injury.

"Whatever." Chris rolled his eyes and bounced back against the seat.

Suddenly, Darci remembered seeing a similar

black SUV parked down the street from her and Chris's place, in front of the blue split-level. The one with a neatly landscaped front yard she envied, and a couple of acres behind it. At least, it looked like the same SUV, with an Honor Student bumper sticker.

Darci pulled up beside the Ford and rolled down her window.

"Hi," she said. "Need some help?"

Jordan looked sheepish. "Thanks, we're fine."

Darci noted he had a little girl—his daughter?—with him. The kid was cute, with long, light brown hair and big blue eyes.

"You don't look fine," Darci said.

He shrugged. "I picked up a nail—" he gestured toward the flat "—and, uh, apparently I didn't maintain my spare tire very well. It's low on air." He glared at his cell phone. "And I'm not getting a signal in this spot for whatever reason."

"Mountains," Darci said, pointing to the surrounding peaks. "My service comes and goes in the oddest places."

"Reception's normally pretty good here." He shrugged. "Maybe it's the weather."

"Need a lift to the gas station?"

"It's closed." He grunted. "Believe it or not, Harry—the owner—took off for the Labor Day holiday weekend to go fishing. You'd think he'd stick around for the tourists coming through."

"How about the convenience store? They have an air pump, don't they?"

Jordan's face went instantly pale, and Darci thought for a minute he was going to pull the same fainting stunt she had done in the E.R. earlier.

"You okay?"

"Not there," he said.

"Pardon?"

"I don't use the convenience store."

"O-kay. Oh, wait. I forgot. I've got a portable compressor in my trunk." She'd bought it for the four-hour road trip when she and Chris had moved here. "I'll pump up your spare for you."

"I'll do it," he said. "Thanks."

"Okay. Let me turn around and park. Be right back." Once more, Darci drove down the street and found a place to change direction, then pulled in behind Jordan.

A honey locust tree grew near the edge of the curb where she'd parked, its overhanging branches offering shelter from the steady rain. That way she could leave the windows down to let in some air. The rain had turned the August evening muggy. "If it gets too stuffy in here, Chris, you can get out," she said.

"Can't I walk home?"

"No. You can wait. Stop being rude."

"Whatever." He stuck his earbuds in and slumped down in the seat again.

From her trunk, Darci retrieved the portable air compressor. Compact in size, it plugged into a vehicle's cigarette lighter. Still, Jordan reached to take it for her as she neared the Explorer. His hand brushed hers, and Darci bit her lip.

"Thank you," he said. "Michaela and I appreciate it."

"No problem." She grinned. "It's the least I can do to return the favor of you stitching up my noggin."

He chuckled, and the sound washed over her, much warmer than the rain.

Jordan had lowered the spare tire rack from underneath the vehicle and removed the thick-treaded radial, laying it on its side. While he hooked up the compressor to an accessory adaptor beneath the SUV's dashboard, Darci clamped the air hose onto the spare. As she straightened back up, she glanced inside the vehicle and frowned. The huge SUV was equipped with enough seats for seven people, yet they were all folded down, except for the two up front. It was as though Jordan Drake and his daughter were the only people who rode in it. Did he have a wife? she wondered again.

The cargo area was practically bare, other than a couple of odds and ends—a small tool box, a pair of kids' tennis shoes, a rope like the kind you might use on a boat.

Odd.

Why would anyone bother to drive such a big, environmentally unfriendly vehicle if they weren't going to utilize its potential? Darci realized Michaela was staring at her over the back of the passenger seat, and she smiled at the girl, giving her a small wave. Michaela smiled back shyly and returned the wave with a lift of her hand, then turned to face forward once again.

Darci couldn't help but notice the scar on the child's face and wondered what had happened. Had she been in a car accident? Cute kid. She seemed about Christopher's age.

"Looks kind of bare, doesn't it?"

Jordan's voice startled her as he stepped up beside Darci.

She hadn't meant to be nosy. "No—it—I was just admiring your SUV."

He gestured toward the folded up seats. "Michaela and I are the only ones who usually ride in it."

The words were casual, but his voice sounded oddly strained, and Darci couldn't help but wonder if there was something he wasn't saying. Just because he and his daughter were the only two who used the SUV didn't mean he had to fold the other seats down, did it? Darci found the situation odd but shrugged it off.

Jordan crouched beside the Ford to keep track of the air compressor's progress, watching the attached dial gauge.

It would take a good fifteen to twenty minutes for the tire to fill, and Darci was getting wet. She wondered if she could go back to sit in her car, or if that would seem rude.

After all, Jordan was getting pelted by the rain, too.

"Have you got a jack?" she asked, opting to stay and help. "I can remove the other tire if you want."

"I'll get it," he said, "but you don't need to stand out here getting wet. I can do it."

"I don't mind," she said.

Jordan went around to the front of the SUV and took a scissor jack from beneath the hood. Returning, he slid it underneath the SUV and crawled after it to adjust the jack's position, then wriggled back out. Crouching again, he twisted the jack handle clockwise, raising the frame to lift the flat off the ground.

A sudden bang startled her, and for a split second, Darci thought the radial had overinflated and blown up. Involuntarily, she let out a little shriek—just as Jordan flung himself against her, shielding her body with his own.

What the…?

Darci grimaced self-consciously as she realized the loud noise had come from an old pickup truck that had driven past and backfired. Silly her. She glanced up into Jordan's face, prepared to apologize for shrieking.

He was sweating so profusely even the rain couldn't hide it. And the fear that crossed his features was so intense.…

What on earth?

"You okay?" Darci asked. "It was only a truck backfiring."

Looking embarrassed, Jordan took a step back. "Sorry," he said gruffly. Without another word, he turned his attention to removing the flat. "You might as well get out of the rain. No sense in us both getting wet."

"Okay. Sure."

Darci sat in her car, pondering what had just happened. Lost in thought, she nearly jumped when Jordan tapped on her window.

"All set," he said.

Darci got out of the car. He'd already put away his tools and had the cord and hose wrapped neatly in place around her air compressor. She reached for it, but he held it aloft.

"I'll get it." Jordan carried the compressor to

the back of the car. Darci popped the truck so he could set it inside. "Thanks again," he said. "I really appreciate your stopping. Guess I'll see you at the hospital."

"Yeah, sure." She watched as he trotted through the rain and climbed into the Explorer.

Belatedly, Darci realized she'd forgotten to tell him they were neighbors.

SATURDAY MORNING DARCI dressed in blue jeans, cowboy boots and a dark brown Resistol, and she and Christopher headed for the Shadow S. Stella had more requests for riding lessons than she could handle, considering she also ran a barrel-racing clinic, and had been happy to hire Darci on as her part-time help.

Anxious for her first day on the job, Darci parked near the barn and got out. Even Christopher was in high spirits. He hadn't been horseback riding on the Shadow S since he was in grade school and had only ridden a few times at the boarding stables outside Northglenn where Darci had worked. He'd gotten to the point where he'd shown little interest in riding at all, and Darci was glad to see him wanting to get back in the saddle.

Over Chris's protests, she had used some of her savings and taken her son shopping that morning. Leon and Stella had rules, and one of them was: no boots, no riding. A tennis shoe could slip through a stirrup and hang a rider up if he fell. People had been killed that way.

And Darci had insisted her son get a pair of jeans that didn't bag halfway down his butt. He'd grumbled as if she were sentencing him to jail, but now he didn't appear to mind wearing the Levi's and cowboy boots she'd purchased at the local feed store.

Leon was cleaning stalls when they arrived. He wore his usual gray cowboy hat, battered boots, faded jeans and flannel shirt. His silver handlebar mustache made him look like he belonged back in the 1800s.

"Hey, kids!" he called, still thinking of Darci that way. "You ready to start your first day, kiddo?" With one meaty hand, he grasped the shovel he'd been using and leaned it against the side of the stall before shifting his six-foot, three-inch frame into the aisle.

"You'd better know it," Darci said. "Chris, you make sure you listen to your uncle today or no riding."

"Aw, he'll be fine," Leon said before Christopher could protest. "Help me finish these stalls, Chris, and we'll be off."

Chris grimaced. "Me, clean up horse crap? I don't think so."

"You want to ride, you help Uncle Leon,"

Darci said. "Having horses isn't all fun and games."

"I don't *have* a horse," he said, making Darci want to shake him.

"No, but you're going to ride one—*if* you help."

"Fine." He shuffled over and took hold of a rake.

Darci blew out a puff of air that lifted her bangs, mentally counting to ten. "Listen to Uncle Leon," she repeated. "Kick him in the butt if he doesn't," she added to her uncle.

Leon only chuckled. "He'll be fine."

Was she overreacting to Chris's attitude? Darci wondered. She didn't think so.

She found Stella saddling a chestnut mare, her short, red hair tucked under her own cowboy hat, the sleeves of her Western shirt rolled up. A short time later, Darci was mounted on the chestnut and in the arena with her first student— a ten-year-old girl named Jodi. The hour-long lesson flew by, and Darci was heading to the office in the barn to get herself some bottled water when another car pulled up outside the stables.

A pretty woman in her mid to late thirties got out and smiled at Darci. She wore boots, jeans and a T-shirt with a picture of a quarter horse on it, her strawberry-blond hair caught up in a ponytail beneath a ball cap.

"Hi. I'm Nina Drake. Is Stella here?"

Darci was taken by pleasant surprise. "Nina— I'm Darci Taylor. My son, Christopher, has an appointment scheduled with you for Thursday."

"Oh, hello." Nina held out her hand. "Nice to meet you, Darci." She pushed back the stray hairs that had escaped her ponytail. "I've been puttering around at the rental stables in town, doing a little riding for relaxation, but I think I need help to hone my skills. I'm here for my first riding lesson with your aunt."

"Sounds like a plan. Follow me. Stella's in the arena out back."

The Shadow S boasted two arenas, the one where Darci had been giving a lesson and one behind the barn. She steered Nina in the right direction, then got her water and prepared for her next student.

By the end of the day Darci was tired in a good way and ready to go home and soak in a hot bubble bath.

She drove on autopilot, chatting with Chris, fully unprepared for what greeted her as she pulled into the driveway of the house they'd moved into just five days ago. Darci stared at the single word of graffiti spray-painted in red across the garage door.

Leave!

Angry tears stung her eyes. This couldn't be happening. No one besides her aunt and uncle knew what Christopher had done—or at least she'd thought so. The local news had covered the story on all channels, but as a minor, Chris's name had been left out, both on television and in the newspapers.

But why else would someone paint the word on their garage door?

Who would be so quick to judge her and her son with such hatred? Her landlord would be livid. And here she'd always thought of the little Colorado mountain town of River's End as peaceful, welcoming.

"Holy crap!" Christopher exclaimed. His face clouded over. "I told you we shouldn't have moved here."

Darci only shook her head. She went inside the house and put her cowboy hat on the closet shelf, then changed into a faded old shirt before going back outside. She entered the garage via the side door and rummaged through some boxes she hadn't yet unpacked, Chris tagging at her heels. Tears stung her eyes. She would not let some stranger's horrible actions get to her.

"Paint thinner, paint thinner…" she mumbled. Had to be here with the other odds and ends she'd brought with her for household repairs. There.

Darci lifted the container from the box, along with some clean rags and a pair of rubber gloves. She'd have to make a trip to the hardware store and get a can of matching yellow paint to completely obliterate the word. Suddenly she felt angry, and that anger was directed at Christopher.

Her own child had made her life a living hell, and she'd had enough. Every penny of her small nest egg was meant to carry her and Chris along until she had a steady paycheck coming in. And now because of her son's stupid actions and some hateful vandal, she had to waste money on paint for what had been a perfectly fine garage door just this morning. Who had had the nerve to do this in broad daylight anyway?

Biting her lip to keep her tears and frustration at bay, Darci tossed the rag at her son. "Here. Clean that off."

"Why do I have to clean it?"

"Maybe because you're the reason for it," Darci snapped, then took a deep breath at the stricken look on her son's face. "Chris, I'm sorry. Christopher!" But he was already pushing his way through the screen door to the house, letting it slam behind him. "Chris!"

He ignored her. Since his father had left a year

ago, Christopher had changed from a quiet boy who loved to read, hike and skateboard to a troublesome young man Darci barely recognized as the child she'd given birth to. These past couple of days, he'd seemed more like his old self again, settling in to their new home better than she'd hoped—or so she'd thought.

Silently, Darci berated herself for directing her anger at him. He was still her son. She got to work with the rag and paint thinner. To her surprise, Christopher came back outside with a larger rag in his hand.

"I'm sorry, Chris," she repeated. "I shouldn't have said that to you. I just can't believe trouble has followed us here so fast."

"It'll never stop," Chris said, his face nearly as red as the paint he viciously scrubbed. "I made one dumb mistake, and now—"

"It will stop," Darci said. It had to, or she'd lose her mind. "We have to believe that. It's just going to take a little time."

He grunted. "I doubt that." He indicated the smeared graffiti. "No one wants us here. We could move to China and everybody would still hate me."

"No one hates you," Darci said, wishing she could believe her own words. For one moment, Christopher looked like the little boy she used to cradle in her lap when he skinned his elbow riding his bicycle. "People are afraid of what they don't understand, and sometimes they react in inappropriate ways."

"Now you sound like Dr. Kingsley." That was Chris's psychologist in Northglenn, who'd referred them to Nina Drake.

"Hey, don't forget you've got me. And Aunt Stella and Uncle Leon." Darci's father had left her mother when Darci was a child, and her mother hadn't been a very good grandmother to Christopher. But then, she lived in California and mostly only saw him on the occasional holiday. Likewise, his father's parents were too busy with their fishing business for Chris. "Now come on, let's not let some jerk spoil our weekend."

Darci worked beside the son she loved, no matter what he'd done. She hated having to uproot him from everything familiar. From the place where he'd lived most of his life…from the people he knew…

The move hadn't been any easier on her than it had on him. But what choice did she have?

No one in the Denver area wanted a kid in their neighborhood who had taken a realistic-looking gun to school and terrified a cafeteria full of students.

CHAPTER THREE

JORDAN DRAKE SLOWED his SUV as he passed
the pale yellow house in the middle of his quiet,
tree-lined block. The house had been vacant up
until a few days ago, but now a petite woman
with short blond hair and a young boy were
busy scrubbing what looked like graffiti from
the door of the attached garage.

Darci? Unlikely. But as she turned in profile,
he recognized her—and that was her little red
Chevy parked in the driveway. He'd had no idea
she lived down the street from him.

He frowned at the graffiti. They'd already
wiped away part of it, but Jordan could make
out what was left of the word *leave.*

What was that all about?

"Dad, someone moved into Mimi's old house,"
Michaela said. "Oh, my gosh, it's the lady who
helped us with our tire yesterday."

"It sure is."

"Dang! Someone graffitied her garage door.
Who would do that in River's End?"

"I don't know, honey."

Crime happened everywhere.

A sudden thought hit Jordan. When the previous tenant—Mimi Hopkins—had lived in the rental house, he'd painted that very garage door for her. In fact, he and Michaela had done the entire exterior of the house and garage for their eighty-year-old neighbor to help her save a little money. Her landlord had agreed to give Mimi a month's free rent if she looked after the much-needed paint job.

When his neighbor had moved to the assisted-living apartments in town, Jordan had forgotten all about the half gallon of yellow paint still in his shed. Until now.

He slowed the Explorer and pulled halfway into Darci's drive. She looked up, then laid down the rag she was holding.

He lowered the window as she approached the driver's side door, her hand cupped over her brow to shade her eyes from the afternoon sun.

"Hi, there," she said, then grimaced. "We had an uninvited visitor."

"So I see. How would you like some free paint to cover that up with?"

She raised her brows. "You have some?" Then quickly added, "I'll pay you for it."

"No need." He shrugged. "I painted this house for the woman who used to live here. I've still got about a half gallon of that pale yellow sitting in my shed. I don't need it. You might as well put it to good use."

She bit her bottom lip, obviously hesitant to accept his offer.

"Consider it repayment for helping me with my tire," he said, before she could protest.

"That's not necessary," Darci said. "I didn't expect any payment."

"I know." He smiled. "I'll go get the paint. Be right back." He raised the window, relishing the air conditioning as he put the SUV in Reverse. This late in the day, and the temperature was still rising. Or was it just the way he felt, being so close to Darci?

Idiot, Jordan chided himself. He hadn't dated in so long—maybe it was Darci's pretty, blue eyes and cute smile that was affecting him. Or the vanilla perfume she wore. He'd noticed it at the hospital and again when he'd reacted to the sound of the truck backfiring, pressing his body against hers.

She'd felt warm and soft, her smooth skin damp from the rain. Her blond hair was wet, curling a little on the ends. He'd felt a quick rush of attraction right before it was replaced by embarrassment at his overreaction to the noise.

You're losing your mind, Drake. Just get the paint.

He told Michaela what he was doing, then walked out to the shed, feeling a strange kind of anticipation at the thought of seeing Darci again.

Chewy ran out of the doghouse to greet him, and he paused to scratch the dog behind one ear. The gallon bucket of "lemon ice" was right where he'd left it last spring, sitting on a shelf along the shed's far wall. He wondered if Darci had a brush or roller. Probably not. Jordan gathered a paint pan, stir stick, an old screwdriver to open the lid and a clean roller, before heading back outside.

He hesitated. *A tarp.* She'd need one to keep from splattering her driveway. Might as well bring his own along, in case she didn't have one. He opened the driver's door of his SUV and reached inside to flip the lever beside the seat, raising the hatch. Jordan placed the paint supplies inside, intending to return to the shed for a tarp. For a moment, he stood without moving, staring at the vast, mostly empty cargo space. His stomach churned as Sandra's voice came to him clearly in memory.

Let's get the seven-seater, babe. I want to fill the thing with kids and soccer balls and football equipment and ballet shoes...

He'd laughed at her enthusiasm. Sandra had been brave and optimistic, no matter what life

had thrown at her. She'd suffered a miscar-
riage prior to Michaela's birth, and two more
afterward. But as Michaela's tenth birthday approached, she'd begun to talk about adopting,
quickly catching Jordan up in her excitement.
With their daughter growing so fast, Sandra was
already dreading the day they'd have an empty
nest, and she'd wanted to do something about
it.

Jordan slammed the hatch shut.

After her death, he'd folded every one of the
five extra passenger seats down, leaving only
the two in front for him and Michaela. The only
time he raised the other rows was if Michaela
had friends along. But afterward he laid the seats
back down, not wanting the reminder of what
should have been. He'd thought about selling the
Explorer, but it was handy in the harsh, snowy
conditions winter often brought to River's End,
and for pulling his cabin cruiser. Plus he hadn't
wanted to upset his daughter with yet another
change. She and her mother had loved the big,
black SUV.

Shaking off his thoughts, Jordan got the tarp
and drove back to Darci's.

Christopher was in the driveway on a skateboard when Jordan pulled back in. The kid
glanced his way, then pushed off down the
sidewalk. Jordan had barely gotten out of the

vehicle when Darci's next door neighbor—Eileen Hathaway—strode across her front lawn in Chris's direction. Eileen's enormous black Newfoundland bounded ahead of the older woman, barking at the boy.

Christopher halted the skateboard and faced the monstrous dog without a bit of fear. The kid's face lit with a smile, and he reached out to ruffle the dog's thick fur. The Newfoundland slobbered all over him, lapping at his hands and wrists with a tongue as long and wide as a two-lane highway.

"Saylor, come here!" Eileen called. "You, too, young man!" Appearing not to notice Jordan or Darci, who'd been waiting near the garage, Eileen focused on Christopher as he turned his board around and reluctantly came back her way.

"It is against the law to ride a skateboard on the sidewalk," Eileen scolded, grabbing hold of Saylor's collar. She shook her finger at Chris, causing the loose skin above her elbow to jiggle. "I heard about what you did in Denver, and if you don't stop roaring past my house on that thing, I'm going to call the police."

Christopher smirked. "Fine." With some fancy footwork, he popped the board into the air, carried it into the street where Darci's car was parked, and set it back down, hopping on again. "I'm not on the sidewalk."

"Christopher!" Darci strode forward but the boy had already taken off.

Eileen turned to glare at Darci. "You need to discipline that boy," she said, her gaze raking Darci judgmentally. "From what I just heard, a trip to the woodshed might do him some good!" With that, she flounced up the steps, tugging poor Saylor along, and slammed the front door shut behind her.

"We don't have a woodshed!" Darci called after her, echoing her son's sarcasm. "Argh." She pushed one hand through her bangs, whirling to face Jordan. The look of surprise and despair in her eyes got to him. "How did she—" Darci began, then shook her head. "Never mind." She helped him with the painting supplies as he took them from the cargo space.

"Don't let her get to you," Jordan said, wondering what exactly Eileen had meant by her comment. What had Chris done that had the woman so upset? Did it have anything to do with the spray-painted graffiti? "Eileen yells at everyone's kid. She reamed Michaela out a while back for letting our dog pee on the grass near the curb when Mac took Chewy for a walk. And yet she owns a dog big enough to poop buffalo chips."

"Yeah, well at least everyone in town isn't gossiping about your daughter," Darci said. "Sorry." She pressed her fingers to both temples. "I'm just thinking out loud."

"You want to talk about it?" he asked.

"I've got to go find Chris. Thank you for everything, though. I'll get your stuff back to you later today."

"No problem." He waited as she ducked inside the house to retrieve her car keys. "Call me if you need anything."

There he went again. But she obviously did need someone to talk to.

Darci nodded, then drove off.

Jordan stood for a moment in the driveway, still holding the bucket of paint. He eyed the garage door. Darci had enough on her hands, and he had a little extra time. It wouldn't take more than a few minutes to paint the door.

Opening the can of yellow, he stirred it, telling himself he wasn't doing this because he was attracted to her. He was simply being a good neighbor. It bugged him that he found her attractive and that he'd seen something in Christopher's expression when the boy interacted with Eileen's dog. A change in his mannerism that gave Jordan the impression of a nice kid longing for something.…

He hadn't been able to save Sandra from the

shooter who'd taken her life. He hadn't been able to protect his little girl from the injuries she'd sustained that cold December day nearly two years ago, or from the psychological fallout of watching her mother die.

So why did he feel the need to reach out to Darci and Christopher?

Using the roller, Jordan hurriedly painted the section of Darci's garage door that had been covered by graffiti, going over it a couple of times to make sure it blended into the older paint.

Then he poured the excess paint back into the can, sealed the lid, and left it beside the garage door in case Darci needed it later. He had no use for the yellow and had only kept it in case Mimi needed a little touch-up work.

Folding the canvas tarp, he loaded it and the paint supplies into his vehicle and drove home.

DARCI DIDN'T HAVE TO LOOK far to find Christopher. He was at the skate park a few blocks away, practicing tricks on the half-pipe. The park was located in an area of town that had once been farmland and open country. As more and more construction occurred, the city limits of River's End had gradually encroached on the wilderness, eating up hillsides of sagebrush and trees, though the town still retained its rural character. It was just no longer the place Darci remembered.

The town had grown by leaps and bounds since her last visit a few years ago. The population had been only six hundred when she was a kid. She'd loved coming here summers to visit her aunt and uncle on their ranch after her parents had moved their family to Denver when Darci was nine.

Which reminded her—she'd invited Stella and Leon over for a barbecue this evening to celebrate the holiday weekend. She needed to get home and paint the garage door, and do some more unpacking so the house would look presentable.

And Christopher was darned sure going to do his share of the work, including the paint touch-up.

He glanced up as she parked at the curb, but kept right on skating on the neon-green board. Darci couldn't help but notice three other boys about his age with skateboards, hanging around the park's perimeter. The trio kept looking Chris's way, as though debating whether or not to approach him.

Darci wished he'd make some friends. If her neighbor knew about what Chris had done at his old school, had other people in town found out, too? Darci swallowed over the scratchy lump in her throat. What had the world come to, when a child could be bullied and harassed over the Internet to the point of being pushed to do something completely outside his nature? Cyberbullying was on the rise, and her son had become just another statistic.

Unfair. Yet they had to deal with it.

Surely Chris would make friends with *someone* at his new school, someone who wouldn't prejudge him. He'd enrolled in River's End Middle School a few days after the school year started, but that couldn't be helped. Darci had gotten them into the rental house as quickly as possible, once it had become available. She'd also had to wait for Christopher to serve out the four-month sentence the juvenile-court judge had rendered before making big changes in their lives.

At least Chris hadn't missed out academically, since Darci had been homeschooling him ever since he'd been expelled from North Star Middle School in Northglenn in the middle of the school year.

She'd thought putting him back in the public school system this year would be good for him. The family counselor they'd been seeing in Northglenn had advised it, as had Christopher's psychologist, both of them agreeing Chris had to learn to make friends again, to fit in with society. *Basically, play well with others,* Darci thought as she tapped the horn, then motioned for Christopher to come to the car. He ignored her, running the skateboard up and down the cement bowls.

Her patience frayed, Darci got out of the car.

"Chris!" she called, walking over to stand near one of the ramps. "Let's go. You've got work to do."

"Can't I stay awhile longer?" Sulkily, he looked at her as he brought the board to a halt. "The garage door isn't going anywhere."

"Nope. Work first, play later. Besides, I don't want people seeing that mess, so come on."

Grumbling, he got into the car, and Darci did her best to ignore the sneers on the faces of the other kids. She hated having to embarrass her son, but he was the one who'd taken off without permission. Of course, at his age even walking through the mall with her could classify as embarrassing in Chris's eyes, depending on the mood he was in. She longed for the days when he was a little boy who needed her, and the worst of her worries was making sure he didn't wander out of sight, or decide to draw a mural on his bedroom wall with a pack of crayons.

He still needs you.

But what had happened to the boy who'd loved

to read about Harry Potter and go hiking and horseback riding with his great aunt and uncle in the mountains, happily helping them out in the stables?

"By the way," Darci said. "I don't want you mouthing off to Mrs. Hathaway anymore."

"Why? She's a nosy old bat."

Darci struggled for control. "That may be. But she's our neighbor, and if we're ever going to fit into this town and have people accept us, we need to show them that we're nice people who are above pettiness. So be polite to the old bat." She looked at him from the corner of her eye and saw him trying not to smile. "All right?"

"Okay." He pulled his iPod from his pocket.

"And it wouldn't hurt to apologize, either."

Chris paused, his earbuds halfway to his head. "You've got to be kidding."

"Nope. Maybe you can take that big ol' dog of hers a treat. A peace offering, say some leftovers from our barbecue tonight? I'll wrap up some cobbler or potato salad or something for Mrs. Hathaway, as well."

"How about a dose of arsenic. For her, not the dog."

"Chris, that's not funny."

"Why not? Everyone thinks I'm a mass murderer anyway."

"Don't you think you're blowing things out of proportion?"

"Mom, someone painted *leave* on our garage. Hell-o."

"Well, you know they're wrong about us, and I know they're wrong. Now let's show them."

"Fine."

They reached the house, and as soon as Darci pulled up in front, she spotted the paint can—and immediately noticed Jordan had already taken care of the garage door for her.

"How about that," Chris smirked. "Guess I don't have to paint the garage after all."

Darci knew Jordan had meant well—still, his actions riled her, especially in her present mood. Didn't he realize she'd wanted Chris to help?

"Go finish writing your report," she said.

"Thrills-ville." Chris strode to the house.

While it was nice of Jordan to loan her the supplies, Darci wished he'd simply left the stuff. And to make matters worse, he'd forgotten the can of paint he'd brought over. Now she'd have to face him when she was annoyed with him.

Or was she more annoyed with herself for finding him hot?

The imp in her head was back.

Darci picked up the gallon can and strolled down the walkway, her palms growing damp at the thought of seeing Jordan again, which only irritated her further.

Michaela answered when she rang the bell. She peered at Darci from behind the partially opened door, safety chain in place.

"Hi, sweetie. Is your dad here?"

"Just a minute." Michaela closed the door in her face, and Darci heard the distinct sound of a dead bolt sliding into place.

What the heck?

She could understand safety precautions, especially having lived in the Denver area, but here in River's End? Had things changed that much in recent years with the town's growth? Or had Michaela not recognized her? No, she'd just seen Darci a short time ago.

The door opened again, this time without the safety chain, and Jordan stood framed in the entryway. "Hi there. What's up?"

"You forgot your paint," she said, holding out the can.

"No, I didn't. I meant for you to keep it, in case you need it for further touch-ups."

"Are you insinuating someone might graffiti my garage again?" Darci knew she was being crabby.

"I hope not," Jordan said. "I only meant you might need it sometime down the road. Scrapes and dings, peeling paint…" He shrugged. "I don't need it. Like I said, I got it for Mimi when she lived in your house."

"Fine. Thank you." Darci tried not to notice how good he looked in his boots and faded jeans. "However, I wish you hadn't done the paint job for me. I'd intended to make Christopher do it as punishment."

"Oh?" He looked curiously at her. "Sorry about that. I just wanted to help."

Suddenly Darci felt contrite for being short with him. It hit her that he had no way of knowing that Christopher's actions were behind the graffiti.

"Okay. Well, thanks again for the paint." Darci could see Michaela hovering behind her father, listening to their every word. Remembering how the kid had bolted the door so abruptly, Darci wanted to put the little girl at ease.

"How are you, Michaela? You know, you don't have to lock the door next time I come over," she teased. "I'm not planning to rob you of your silverware or anything."

Michaela gasped loud enough for Darci to hear. Then she covered her mouth and turned to hurry up the stairs with her cane, clinging to the railing for support.

"Mac!" Jordan called, turning to watch his daughter. When he faced Darci again, his dark eyes were filled with a mixture of sadness and irritation.

What had she said?

"I—I'm sorry." Darci was truly perplexed. "I didn't mean to upset her. It's just that she closed and chained the door while she went to get you." She shrugged. "This neighborhood's pretty safe, isn't it? River's End isn't exactly the center of crime."

Jordan's features tensed. "It's not as safe as you think," he said. "See you later, Darci." With that, he closed the door.

Darci stood there, her mouth literally hanging open.

She wasn't sure what rattled her more. The fact that she'd somehow upset Michaela, or that Jordan had practically slammed the door in her face.

What *had* she said?

Darci plunked the can of paint down on the porch, turned and headed home.

CHAPTER FOUR

THE LINGERING AROMA of barbecue smoke drifted pleasantly around the patio as Darci sat with Stella at a small folding table, enjoying one last hamburger. At the back of the garage, her uncle Leon shot hoops with Chris, having coaxed the boy into a game of horse after Christopher had wolfed down two hamburgers and three hot dogs.

"You've got paint on your nose," Stella said. "Right there." She indicated the bridge of Darci's nose. "What were you painting?"

Darci used a paper napkin to wipe the spot away. It must have gotten there when she put away the paint. "The garage door." She sighed. She hadn't wanted to bring up the incident in front of Chris. She'd hoped to enjoy the barbecue and forget that someone didn't want them here in River's End. "Somebody sprayed graffiti on it."

"Taggers?" Stella asked. "In River's End?" She shook her head. "What's this world coming to?"

"Not taggers," Darci said. "Someone painted

leave on my garage in big, red letters. Why would they do that, unless they know what Christopher did. And how could they? His name was never on the news."

Stella squirmed uncomfortably. "Well— um—I might've said something about what happened."

Darci's jaw dropped. "Who did you tell?"

"Just Lucy Long, down at Trail's Inn Pizza."

"Oh, Aunt Stella. You know Lucy talks to Suzanne." The owner of the local beauty shop was a renowned gossip. "And if you tell Suzanne, you might as well broadcast it over the local news." That explained how Eileen Hathaway had heard about Chris.

Stella pressed her hand to her forehead. "I'm sorry, Darci. I wasn't thinking. But I only spoke in Christopher's defense, which is exactly what I told Lucy—those kids were cyberbullying him."

Her aunt had a point, but it didn't excuse Chris's actions. With his love of horses and Southern-country rock, he hadn't fit in with the kids at school, not even the other skaters. He'd been teased for the way he dressed, for the music he listened to and for hanging out at the boarding stables with Darci. And the teasing had escalated.

"It'll blow over," Stella said. "You'll see."

"But what's next? What if someone damages my car, or breaks one of our windows? Maybe I should get a guard dog."

"Now, don't go borrowing trouble." Stella's gaze softened as she leaned in close. "I'm sure this was a onetime thing."

"Yeah, well, I wish I felt the same." Darci plunked her half-eaten burger down on her plate, no longer hungry. She had gone through hell in Northglenn. She didn't think she could take another round.

"Everything will work out—you'll see," her aunt assured her.

Darci had her doubts. Especially if Chris kept being such a little shit. She watched him hook a shot using fancy wrist work. A grin spread across his face as he shouted playful abuse at Leon.

He was still her little boy.

"You're worrying too much." Stella reached out and took both of Darci's hands in hers.

The familiar scent of lavender drifted over Darci, taking her right back to her childhood, when her aunt Stella could fix anything with a word of encouragement and some chocolate-chip cookies. If only life were so simple now.

"You know what you need?" Stella said. "To do something fun. There's a horse auction next weekend. Why don't you plan on going with me and Leon? I'm looking for a few more lesson horses, now that I've got you as my partner. You can help me pick 'em out." She gave a wink, and Darci managed a smile.

"Sounds good to me."

"Okay. It's a date. Chris will have a great time."

"I just wish I could help him settle in here and get adjusted."

"Adjusted my tail." Stella waved the thought away like a fly at their cookout. "He's a big boy. Let him adjust on his own."

"Aunt Stella." Darci could hardly believe her aunt would be so callous. "He's been through a lot."

"And so have you. Chris is playing you as sure as he's playing your uncle in that game of horse."

Darci's jaw dropped.

"You heard me. 'Poor me. Poor Chris. Everybody hates Christopher.' The boy made a dumb mistake, but he's done his time, and I'm here to tell you that the sooner you get past all that and let that kid deal with things on his own, the better it will be for both of you. Hell, he'll land on two feet. Just toss him in the air and see if I'm not right."

Darci knew Stella's tough-love approach hid a heart that was as big as the Colorado sky, but still she felt edgy. "I was starting to second-guess my decision to put him back in public school. I wish I could afford to quit work and homeschool him."

"He'll be all right. Anything happens, they'll call you at work. Just like they do any other parent. Let go, Darci. You're going to start meeting people through your job and through the school. Not everyone will be against you. You'll see. Getting out there will help you and Chris become part of the community a lot quicker than if you both hide out at home." She nudged Darci. "Chin up."

Darci nudged her back. "Okay, Aunt Bossy."

"Moo," Stella said, then laughed. "Say, why don't you leave Chris with me and Leon for a couple of days, since it's a long weekend? He can go riding tomorrow…help Leon putter around the place a bit. School's out till Wednesday, right? We can even take him to the fair if he wants."

The county fair was always held over the Labor Day weekend and ran until the middle of the week. Because so many of the local students were also 4-H members who showed livestock, the kids got an extra long holiday from school.

"That would be nice," Darci said. Chris used to love the fair and the ranch…not just riding but mending fences with his great uncle. Would he still?

Stella smiled. "We'll have fun, plus it'll give you a chance to settle into your house."

Could she do this? Darci thought. Start over with her new job, a whole new set of friends? She hoped her aunt was right, that she and Christopher would eventually feel welcome here.

"All right," she said. "Maybe I can get some more unpacking done."

"There you go. So stop frowning."

"Sorry. I'm still a little worried. I just wish I knew who defaced our garage. What if a kid does something to Chris at school?"

Stella bopped Darci on the head with a half-full bag of barbecue chips before clipping the rolled top shut with a clothespin. "Like I said, don't go borrowing trouble, 'cause Lord knows it finds its way to us quick enough."

As if on cue, a red-and-white mottled dog darted out of nowhere into the backyard and snatched a leftover burger from the plate beside the barbecue grill.

"Hey!" Chris shouted. The basketball hit him smack in the face as Leon bounced it his way, realizing too late that Chris wasn't paying attention. His nose started to bleed, but he didn't seem to notice. Instead, he raced off after the dog.

"Christopher!" Darci shouted. But if he heard her, he ignored her. *Nothing new there.*

She got up and ran down the block after him, calling his name again.

"She's got puppies," he said over his shoulder, as if that explained everything.

What on earth?

Feeling every one of her thirty-five years, Darci lagged behind as the mama dog scurried into a yard a few houses down.

Oh, boy.

Her pulse picked up speed.

It was Jordan's yard, and the dog raced around to the back of the house.

Chris hesitated only a moment before turning up the front walk.

"Christopher Lee, you stop right now!"

Something in her voice must've told him she meant business, because Chris stopped and turned to face her, jogging impatiently in place. "Come on, Mom! She's got *pups.*"

He'd been bugging her for a puppy when they lived in Northglenn, and she'd pacified him by saying they might be able to get a dog once they moved, *if* his behavior improved. And she'd told Stella she was considering getting a dog. But a guard dog, not a puppy.

As Darci stopped to catch her breath, Chris

opened the chain-link gate and headed up the walk, clearing the porch steps then knocking on Jordan's door.

JORDAN CHOPPED FRESH cilantro, whistling as the knife thumped against the cutting board. Tacos were his daughter's second favorite behind pizza, and he enjoyed making them, complete with his own homemade salsa. He was glad Michaela had invited Jenny over for supper and to spend the night. It would take her mind off the earlier incident with Darci.

A knock sounded at the door and he figured it was Jenny. "Michaela!" he called, sliding the cilantro from the cutting board into a bowl.

"I know!" she hollered. She thumped down the steps to the front door and swung it open without the safety chain.

But it wasn't Jenny's voice Jordan heard. It was a boy. Ben? Had Jenny's twin brother come with her for some reason? Wiping his hands on a towel, Jordan started toward the foyer.

"—puppies."

"How do you know my dog has pups?" Michaela's voice held a defensive note. "Were you in our yard?"

"No! Your dog stole a hamburger off our grill."

"She wouldn't."

"She did."

Jordan strode to the door as he recognized the boy's voice.

"Hello, Christopher. What can I do for you?" He could see Darci, hanging back a few steps from the fence. She was wearing denim shorts and a pink tank top and her blond hair was tousled, as if she'd been running. He wasn't sure he liked the way she seemed to stir something inside him, but he waved her into the yard. "Darci, what's up?" Then he noticed Christopher's nose was bleeding. "What happened to you?"

The kid brushed the back of his hand across the smear of blood. "Nothing. I mean, it's no big deal. I—uh—wanted to know if I could see your puppies?"

"Well, Chewy's a little protective of them right now. But you're welcome to come back when they get their eyes open and start walking around. How'd you know about them?"

"I followed your dog. I could tell she's nursing a litter."

"Ah. Sherlock Holmes." Jordan stepped out onto the porch.

"She came into our yard," Darci added, standing beside Christopher now. "And she did steal a hamburger. But it's no big deal."

"I'm sorry," Jordan said. "She's a stray we adopted, so she's not really trained."

"So, how long before their eyes open?" Chris asked, his own eyes wide and eager. "I really want to get a dog."

"About another week. And since you're the first person to ask for one, I guess that means you get pick of the litter."

Michaela scowled, and Jordan put his arm around his daughter's shoulders, wondering what was wrong. She was never unfriendly.

"That is," Jordan added, "if it's all right with your mom." He looked at Darci.

"We'll see," she said. "Chris, we haven't really discussed this."

"Please," he begged, clasping his hands together.

"I said we'll see. Now let's go. Uncle Leon and Aunt Stella are probably wondering where we ran off to." She turned to look at Jordan. "Thanks for the offer. I'll let you know. I hope we didn't disturb you." She hesitantly acknowledged Michaela, no doubt remembering how she'd upset her earlier.

Jordan knew he should explain, but this wasn't the time.

"Not at all," he said. "I'll see you Monday, Darci." No long weekends for hospital staff.

"Yeah," she said. "See you. Bye, Michaela."

"Bye," Michaela said, with obvious reluctance. She turned to go inside.

"Hold up a minute, Mac." Jordan closed the front door behind them. "What's wrong?"

"I don't like them."

Jordan sat down on the couch and patted the cushion beside him. "Why not? You don't even know them."

"And I don't want to." She chewed her lip. "I talked to Jenny earlier, and she told me what Christopher did—why he had to leave his old school." She was shaking now, and Jordan grew concerned.

"What did he do?"

"He took a gun to school and threatened some kids in the lunchroom."

"*What?* Are you sure?" And then he recalled a story that had dominated the news last year. It was about a twelve-year-old boy who'd taken a replica gun to school and scared a cafeteria full of students and teachers. No one was hurt, Jordan recalled, but people were extremely upset about the whole thing. Understandable after the terrible shootings that had occurred at Columbine High School some years ago.

"That's what people at school are saying," Michaela went on. "I don't want him to have one of Chewy's puppies."

"We'll talk about that later," he said. "I'll speak to Chris's mom."

If it really was Christopher who'd threatened his classmates, maybe he'd changed in the months since it happened.

Then again, maybe he hadn't. Jordan's first instinct was to protect his daughter, but at the same time, he couldn't help wonder why Chris would have done something so awful.

He had to have had a reason.

Didn't he?

So that would explain the graffiti, and why Christopher was seeing his sister Nina, a psychologist.

He wished he could ask Nina about the boy, and knowing he couldn't left him feeling restless. There was always the good old gossip mill. Shirley, the hospital receptionist, would likely know something.

Then again, he could always just ask Darci.

THE FOLLOWING SATURDAY, Darci awoke early, anxious for the auction. It would be fun to help Stella and Leon pick out horses. She showered and dressed, then went to wake up Christopher.

"Mo-om," he groaned. "It's Saturday. I want to sleep in."

"Nothing doing, buddy. You're not staying

here alone, and you're not making me miss this auction."

Christopher covered his head with a pillow. "I'm thirteen, for crying out loud! When are you going to stop making me feel like I need a sitter all the time?"

"When I decide you've earned the privilege to stay by yourself. Now get up and get dressed. We'll have fun."

But a part of Darci felt guilty as she left his room. Was she being overprotective, not letting her son stay home alone? She couldn't help it. After all that had happened, she felt she needed to keep a close eye on him. Darci sighed. Maybe Nina Drake could shed some light on the matter. Chris's first appointment with her on Thursday had gone well. He liked Nina, and so did Darci. She'd gotten to know the woman a little better the couple of times she'd seen her at the Shadow S this week, and had made an appointment to talk with her one on one. Darci had some issues of her own that weren't yet resolved, and talking to her son's counselor might benefit both her and Chris.

To Darci's surprise, Christopher actually had on his boots and jeans when she went downstairs. "Hey, you're wearing your boots," she said.

"Might as well. We're going to a horse auction, aren't we?"

"Yes, we are. Now how about some pancakes before we take off?"

Darci made apple-cinnamon pancakes from a mix, and even got Christopher to help clean up the dishes without too much complaining. Then they were off.

The auction barn was located at the edge of town, not far from the feed store. Trucks and trailers were parked everywhere when they arrived in Stella and Leon's extended-cab Chevy, towing a four-horse trailer. Leon found a spot just a few spaces down from a familiar black Ford Explorer.

What would Jordan be doing at the horse auction? But there was the Honor Student bumper sticker, and as Darci walked toward the holding pens out behind the auction barn with Christopher and her aunt and uncle, she found herself looking for Jordan.

It wasn't long before she spotted him. He was with Michaela, checking out the rows of horses fenced off in pipe-rail pens.

"Isn't that Dr. Drake?" Stella asked.

"Yes, it is. I'm going to go over and say hello." Darci brushed past a group of cowboys who'd gathered outside a pen of Appaloosas, and walked down the aisle toward Jordan and Michaela.

"Hey there," she said. "Fancy meeting you here, Doc."

"Hi, Darci." Jordan glanced at her with mock torment. "My daughter dragged me here, our monthly ritual." The auctions were held the first Saturday of every month. "She's determined to talk me into buying her a horse, but I'm not sure my nerves can take putting my kid on the back of an eleven-hundred-pound beast. For today, we're just looking. Isn't that right, snicker-doodle?"

"But we might find a good, safe horse this time, Dad," Michaela said. "One you can't resist." She smiled shyly at Darci and said hi.

"And you?" Jordan asked. "You horse shopping?"

"Sort of. I'm here with my aunt and uncle. They're looking for lesson horses."

"Ah. Well, there sure are a lot to choose from, aren't there?"

"A lot of head, that's for sure," Darci said. "But you've got to be careful you don't pick a lemon."

He laughed. "Kind of like buying a used car off the lot, eh?"

"Something like that." Darci willed her heart to stop beating so fast. Jordan looked handsome in his usual boots and jeans, a ball cap perched low over his espresso eyes. "You know, before you think about buying Michaela a horse, you might want to consider letting her take some riding lessons. It might help ease your apprehension, and Aunt Stella and I give lessons out at the Shadow S. We'd be happy to have her." She smiled at the girl.

And obviously won a few brownie points.

"Can I, Dad?" Michaela asked, eyes wide and eager.

"Slow down there, kiddo. We'll have to see." He addressed Darci. "We're just here for fun today. Nothing definite yet."

"I understand. Just know she's welcome anytime."

"Thanks. I appreciate it." He nodded toward the sale barn. "Guess we'd better get a seat before all the good ones are taken."

"Right," Darci said. "See you inside." She cringed inwardly, hoping she hadn't overstepped. She'd only meant to help—not make things difficult for Jordan. She knew how it could be, having a kid want something you weren't sure they were ready for. Christopher's earlier plea to stay home alone came to mind.

Darci backtracked and found Stella and Leon. "See any you like?" she asked.

"That little buckskin mare looks promising," Stella said.

"Yeah, and I kind of like the overo paint gelding." Uncle Leon nodded toward the beautifully marked, tricolor paint.

"There's a couple of others we're considering," Stella added. "So what say we get inside before the bidding starts?"

In spite of his earlier grumblings, Christopher seemed to brighten once they had their seats and the horses were being run through the sale ring. Darci knew he loved horses way more than he was letting on.

She glanced around and spotted Jordan and Michaela one row up and a few seats over. She nodded and smiled, and Jordan smiled back and tipped the bill of his ball cap at her.

Darci felt herself blush all the way to her toes. Dear God, the man was good-looking!

She faced forward, concentrating on the horses. When the buckskin mare came up, Stella made a bid, and ended up buying her for a fair price. But when the overo paint's turn rolled around, Leon was outbid by a cowboy seated near the corral-like enclosure where the horses were being auctioned off.

"Well, darn it," Leon said. "Guess I'll try for the next one on my list of picks."

Following the tricolored paint, a black mare that looked to be a quarter horse was run into the ring. She seemed shy, spooking a little at the crowd, but something about her caught Darci's attention. The horse's ebony coat was shiny in spite of the fact that she was underweight, and her wide, brown eyes seemed kind even if she was a bit skittish at all the activity around her.

"That mare looks nice," Darci said, leaning over to speak to her aunt. "She's got a pretty head."

"Nice conformation, too," Stella said.

The auctioneer gave a brief description of the mare, who turned out to be only five years old, then started the rapid-fire bidding.

The older cowboy sitting on the opposite side of Leon spoke loudly enough for Darci to hear. "That mare's been abused. I know the people she came from. They didn't feed her right, and any-time the fella's temper flares when he's working a horse, he takes it out on the animal."

Immediately, Darci's back went up. Who could abuse such a beautiful animal? Or any animal for that matter. "She looks so sweet," she said, leaning toward her aunt and uncle. "Bid on her, Uncle Leon. I'll help you work with her."

He grinned. "Softie."

She nudged him good-naturedly. "Look who's talking."

"All right. She is a good one, and I think the price will be right." Rumors about the animal's treatment were obviously circling the sale barn, and Darci noticed a few people shaking their heads. Lots of folks didn't want to bother with an animal that would require rehabilitation, but it wouldn't be the first time her aunt and uncle had taken in a horse in need.

Within minutes, Leon had purchased the black mare for a bargain price. Darci looked over her shoulder and caught Jordan's eye. He gave her a wink and a thumbs up, and she returned the gesture.

By the end of the auction, Stella and Leon had acquired two Appaloosa geldings in addition to the buckskin mare and the black quarter horse. Darci and Christopher walked with her aunt and uncle to the office, where Stella wrote a check to pay for the animals, then they all went outside to collect the horses. Christopher seemed particularly animated at the prospect of loading the newly acquired animals into the trailer, and Darci was glad to see him so involved.

"That's a nice black mare."

She turned to find Jordan and Michaela behind her.

"Yeah, she is. I guess she was abused."

Jordan nodded. "I heard that, too." He shook his head. "I'll never understand people."

"That makes two of us." Darci watched as Leon approached the quarter horse. The mare rolled her eyes in fear, pinning her ears in trepidation rather than anger. She whirled around to face the fence, doing her best to avoid Leon and the nylon halter he held.

"Whoa, babe," Leon said in a low, reassuring voice. "There's a girl." Stella joined him, the two of them gently corralling the black into a corner. The mare trembled, but allowed them to approach. Softly, Stella placed her hand on the animal's shoulder, stroking the horse as she talked soothingly to her. After that, it didn't take much for Leon to slip the halter over her head, and the mare walked into the trailer willingly enough.

"Looks like she's a good one," Jordan said.

Darci nodded. "All she needs is a little TLC."

"Well, it was good seeing you, Darci," Jordan said. "Guess we'll head on out."

Darci practically felt the ends of her hair curl at the silky way her name slid over his lips. She said her goodbyes, then caught up with Stella at the truck.

"Looks like someone's sweet on you," Stella said.

"What? No way. He was just being friendly."

"Uh-huh. If you say so." Stella smiled. "Lighten up, Darci. It wouldn't hurt you to go out on a date."

"A date! Who said anything about dating?"

"Well, you're both single, and Lord knows he

could use some fun after what the poor man's been through."

Darci frowned. "What do you mean?"

Stella lowered her voice. "I thought you might've heard. His wife was killed in a robbery two years ago on Christmas Eve."

CHAPTER FIVE

"OH MY GOD." DARCI clamped a hand against her chest. "How awful. What happened?"

"A couple of punks held up the convenience store. Sandra, Jordan's wife, and little Michaela had gone there to get some last-minute items for their Christmas dinner, and they got caught in the crossfire."

Darci gasped.

"That's how Mac injured her hip, and her poor little face was scarred where a gunshot grazed her. She took three bullets, bless her heart. Was in the hospital for the longest time."

"Poor kid." No wonder Jordan hadn't wanted to use the convenience store pump when he'd had the flat last week. Or that Michaela was upset the other day when Darci had ribbed her about locking the front door. "Me and my big mouth."

"What do you mean?" Stella asked.

Darci explained.

"Well, you couldn't have known."

"Still, I feel bad. I want to make it up to her."

"So, offer her a free lesson."

Darci brightened. "That's an idea. Actually, I did mention riding lessons to Jordan. I think he's worried she might get hurt."

"Give him one of these." Stella rummaged around in her purse and came up with a bright blue business card for the ranch. On the back was a coupon good for a free lesson.

"Perfect," Darci said, pocketing the card. "I'm going to grab a hot dog for the road. Want one?"

"I'M THIRSTY, DAD." Michaela stopped in front of the snack booth outside the auction barn. "Can I have a Coke? Maybe some nachos?"

"Boy, I don't know, snicker-doodle. You're eating me out of house and home." Jordan pretended to pat his empty pockets.

Michaela chuckled. "I'm a growing girl, what can I say?"

Jordan walked with her to the snack bar, pleasantly surprised when he spotted Darci there. "We've got to quit meeting like this," he said as Michaela went up to the booth to place her order.

Darci turned to face him, a paper sack of what

smelled like hot dogs in one hand, a drink in the other.

"I thought you'd gone home," she said.

He grinned. "We had an emergency nacho stop."

"Actually, I'm glad I caught you." Darci set the bag down on a nearby table and reached in her pocket. "I wanted you to have this. No obligation." She held out a brightly colored business card after jotting something on it.

Jordan read it. *Her cell number?*

"Turn it over."

He flipped the card.

"Well, that's really nice of you, Darci, but like I said, I'm not sure if I want Mac to take riding lessons."

"No problem. The offer's there if you want it. I wrote down my cell number. We'd love to have your daughter come out to the Shadow S if you change your mind."

"Change your mind about what?" Michaela spoke from behind him and Jordan cringed. He'd thought she was still at the booth.

Before he could answer, Michaela zeroed in on the neon-blue coupon. "Nothing, Mac," he said, attempting to shove the card in his pocket. Of course he dropped it on the ground, and following the law of dropped toast always landing butter side down, the card fell with the coupon offer facing up.

Michaela squealed, diving for the business card. "A free riding lesson! Dad, can I?" She looked eagerly from him to Darci and back again.

Jordan sighed. "We'll see."

"Oh, please, Dad, please!" Michaela could barely stand still.

"I said we'll see," Jordan repeated, suddenly irritated that Darci had even given him the card. He knew she meant well, but...

"Don't worry, the coupon doesn't expire," she said to Michaela. "Your dad is free to take his time."

Well, thank you very much. Then Jordan felt bad. Darci was only trying to be nice.

"We'll let you know," he said. "Now come on, Mac. We've got things to do at home."

"Bye, Darci," she said. "Thanks."

"You're welcome. See you later, Jordan."

He nodded.

Michaela babbled a mile a minute on the drive home about lessons and horses and how much fun she and Jenny could have riding together once she got a horse of her own.

"Whoa, whoa," Jordan said. "Let's not get ahead of ourselves."

"I just wish you'd let me take the free lesson, Dad. Darci seems nice, and so does her aunt."

"Nice? I thought you said you didn't like her and Christopher?"

Michaela's face turned pink. "Well, I don't like what I've heard about Chris. But Darci seems okay. I really, really want to ride, Dad. Will you please think hard about it?"

"I said I would." And Jordan planned to do just that, for as long as he could.

CHRISTOPHER RELISHED THE BREEZE that kicked up and blew across his face as the horse galloped along. A feeling of freedom washed over him.

He hadn't realized how much he'd missed horseback riding. After the auction yesterday, he'd gone home with Aunt Stella and Uncle Leon to spend the night. It was heaven. Just like last weekend. No school. No mom to nag him about unpacking his stuff or painting a garage door. No cranky neighbors to make him feel like crap. Just the wide open space of Colorado's western slope.

Though his muscles were still sore from the long trail ride he and Stella and Leon had taken with the new horses last night, it was a good kind of ache. Chris had lain in bed, remembering the feeling of freedom he'd experienced whenever he'd ridden alone. The last time he'd visited the ranch, he'd been too small and was only allowed to ride in the arena, with his mom. Still, he'd felt such a rush to be on a horse by himself.

So last night he'd made up his mind to get up at the crack of dawn and saddle up Dollar before anyone else was awake. He was afraid if he asked to go out alone, Uncle Leon and Aunt Stella would say no. But he needed some time by himself. He was pretty sure he'd be in the doghouse when they found him gone, even though he'd left a note. Maybe they were looking for him right now. He'd been riding all morning, stopping now and then to give Dollar a rest and a drink from one of the many creeks in the area.

And he'd loved it.

He'd spotted some minnows skittering through the shallows of a stream as he sat waiting for the horse to drink. A doe approached with her half-grown fawn, and Chris had frozen in place, watching the elegant creatures as they switched their tails at the deer flies, staring at him with wide, round eyes. They twitched the big ears that gave them their name, mule deer, trying to determine if he posed a threat. In the end, they'd moved upstream, springing away on pogo-stick legs.

Chris had been enjoying himself so much,

he'd lost track of the time. He knew he should head back to the ranch, but he had one more place to visit—his house. His mother hadn't seen him on a horse in forever, and he wanted her to be proud of him for once. Proud of his abilities. He had another motive, as well. He planned to ride up to Michaela Drake's house and show off a bit. He'd overheard her talking at the auction, and knew that Jenny McAllister was going to be at her house.

He had a crush on Jenny a mile wide, but his face burned every time he thought of the way she looked at him. Like she'd heard all about what he'd done at his old school. He'd show her, and he'd show Michaela. She'd looked down her nose at him as if she didn't want him to have one of her puppies. Like he wasn't good enough or something. No way could Miss Smarty Pants ride a horse, not with her limp and her cane.

Chris felt a flush of remorse, but only for a moment. If Michaela Drake was going to believe rumors about him, he had every right to think mean thoughts about her.

He took the trail that led over the ridge, down the mountain and back toward town, riding the county dirt and gravel roads until he came to the subdivision where he lived. A big meadow stretched behind the block, dotted with sagebrush and rock. Chris jogged Dollar along the dirt and grass shoulder of the quiet street that followed the meadow's edge. As he neared the cross street that would lead to the front of his house, he let his gaze scan the row of backyards.

He hadn't realized that Michaela's backyard led into a large rectangular field partially fenced with barbed wire.

Was the field part of the Drakes' property? If so, Michaela would have room for a horse right in her own backyard and she probably couldn't even ride one with her limp.

If only the rental house he and his mom had moved into had that kind of acreage. Then maybe he could talk his mom into a dog *and* a horse. Surely Uncle Leon would help them pick one out at the auction, or maybe he'd sell one of his and Aunt Stella's quarter horses to Mom. Maybe even Dollar.

But as soon as the idea came to him, Chris realized he was only dreaming. They probably wouldn't even end up getting to stay in the neighborhood the way things were looking.

Oh, well.

Originally he'd intended to ride up to his front yard, but now Chris turned onto the dirt trail that wound along the meadow behind the subdivision, letting Dollar jog until they drew close to Mac's property. He slowed the horse to a walk, riding alongside the barbed wire. Would

Mac and Jenny see him? If not, he'd call their names—get them to come outside.

Suddenly the dog they called Chewy came running out from a doghouse. Barking furiously, she cleared the backyard fence and streaked through the pasture. Chris recognized her as part Australian Cattle Dog. He'd studied the various breeds, reading book after book on dogs when he was younger. Now he pulled up on Dollar's reins and gave a sharp whistle. The dog stopped short, ears erect, eyes alert as she took in the horse and Chris. She acted as though she wanted to heel the gelding, nip at his heels to herd him. She was definitely a red heeler. And that could mean trouble.

Chris pictured himself falling from the saddle if Dollar spooked, not something he wanted Michaela to witness. He was just about to dismount when she appeared in the backyard.

"Chewy!" she called. "Come here."

The dog looked at Dollar, tongue lolling, then back over her shoulder at the girl. Dollar shifted beneath Chris, but didn't appear to be frightened of Chewy. Not yet, anyway. But if she came closer...

"Chewy, come!" Michaela repeated.

Leaning on her cane, she made her way toward the dog, a purse slung over her shoulder as though she'd been about to go somewhere.

Maybe with Jenny? Was she still at Michaela's? He held his breath. Sure enough, just as Michaela was midway across the pasture, Jenny came through the back door, staring at him. Her long, blond hair fell to her waist in a cascade of waves, and Christopher's heart started to pound.

She stared at him, looking no friendlier than Michaela.

Great.

Oh, well, he'd show them.

As the girls drew closer, Chris gathered the reins, then squeezed Dollar with his legs, making the horse dance in place. Dollar was a beautiful animal, his blood bay coat a deep, shiny red, his silky mane and tail as black as a crow's feather. And Aunt Stella and Uncle Leon kept their tack clean and well polished, the silver conchas on Dollar's saddle and bridle gleaming in the noon light.

Chris only wished he was wearing something better than the boots and jeans his mom had made him buy. But Uncle Leon and Aunt Stella had their rules. Still, Chris wasn't a cowboy.

Would Jenny laugh at him for not being a cowboy like her brother Ben? Would she think he was a fake for just wearing the boots? He wanted so badly for her to notice him in a good way.

He let the reins out a little, allowing Dollar to lope. The big horse held his head high, snorting, his stride long and even as he leveled out his gait. "Easy, boy," Chris whispered to him. "That's right. Looking good."

They loped a few yards, then trotted, then Chris turned Dollar back the way they'd come, letting him prance again as he came even with the Drakes' pasture.

"Show off," Jenny called out to him. "What are you trying to prove? That you're a cowboy?"

He was right!

Chris glared at her. "Not hardly."

"Good, because my dad and my brother are real cowboys, and you're nothing like them. I sure didn't see you at the fair last week."

"The fair's lame," Chris fibbed.

"Yeah, whatever." Jenny tossed her pretty, white-blond hair.

She was so cute. Too bad she was being such a witch.

"Wannabe hick," Michaela taunted. "Ew-ww, I'm impressed."

Christopher's anger swelled. *Jealous.* They were only jealous. Dollar was an awesome horse.

"You're the wannabe," he told Michaela. "You wanna be normal and ride." He knew he was being mean, but he was through being picked on. He'd had enough of it back in Northglenn.

He sent Dollar into a quick sprint, then hauled back on the reins. The bay horse tucked his hindquarters and slid, plowing up the dirt in a beautiful sliding stop. *Yep. He still had it.*

"Ohh, look at the Rexall Ranger," Jenny said, hands on hips, wagging her head side to side. "Whoopie."

"Wait," Michaela said, reaching into her purse. "Let me get this on video." She took out a pink cell phone and aimed it at Christopher. "Smile, little cowboy."

Instantly, a queasy feeling gripped Christopher. A memory crashed into his mind of another day and time that his mom knew nothing about....

A kid had taken Chris's cell phone and...
Smile, turd face.

The smell of the school locker room came back to him in a flash. Sweaty tube socks and T-shirts, a hint of soap. And the face of the boy who'd taken Chris's cell phone out of his backpack and used it to make Chris's life a living hell.

"Knock it off!" he screamed as Michaela took his picture. No, a video. Even worse.

"What's the matter, wannabe?" Michaela said.

"You can't be a gangsta or a cowboy? So what are you, a freak?"

Fury surged through Christopher. In one smooth motion, he swung off Dollar's back, dropping the reins to the ground, and lunged at Michaela. The girl's eyes grew wide as he closed in on her and grabbed for the cell phone.

As he tried to yank it from her grasp to delete the video, she let out a scream that pierced his eardrums.

One he was pretty sure the whole neighborhood heard.

And then she tripped over her cane and fell down, taking him with her.

Shit.

DARCI'S CELL PHONE RANG as she pulled into her driveway, home from a short shift at the hospital. The personalized ring tone told her it was Stella. She and Leon were probably ready to have her pick up Chris. Darci only hoped he hadn't been too much trouble, sleeping over at the ranch two weekends in a row.

"Hi, Aunt Stella. What's up? I was just going to change my clothes and head your way."

"You need to get here as soon as you can," Stella said. "We can't find Chris anywhere— we've been out looking for him all morning. Dollar's missing, too."

"He took off on horseback alone?" Darci's pulse picked up. "Why didn't you call me sooner?"

"We didn't want to bother you at work," Stella said. "I really thought we would've found him by now."

"Okay." Darci forced herself to remain calm. *He's out riding. No big deal.* "I'm on my way." She started the car's engine and turned on the air-conditioning.

"Hang on a minute," Stella said. Darci heard her uncle's voice in the background. "Leon just found a note. Breeze from the kitchen window must've blown it off the table. Chris *did* go riding, and at least he told us which trails he took. I feel better now, and I shouldn't have worried you. Dollar's a good, solid horse."

"No, you were right to call," Darci said, the mother in her more than a little concerned. "Even if he did tell you where he was, Chris shouldn't have taken off alone. Up until last weekend, it's been a while since he's done any extensive riding."

"Well, you shouldn't let that bother you, either," Stella reassured her. "He took right back to it like a city duck to a country pond. Leon had him out riding fence last week, and the three of us went for a pretty good trail ride yesterday evening. Chris hasn't lost his touch."

Darci breathed a little easier. "Thanks, Aunt Stella. I'll be there as quick as I can."

She'd no sooner closed the phone than it rang again. Jordan's name popped up on the caller ID. Had he decided to let Michaela take riding lessons after all?

Darci flipped the phone open. "Hey, what's up?"

"I'm afraid Michaela had a run-in with Christopher."

"What are you talking about? Chris is out horseback riding."

"Yeah, I know. He rode over to the house and decided to harass Michaela and her friend Jenny. I was in the basement, but my neighbor, Louise, saw the whole thing. She came running over here. Said Mac and Christopher got into a scuffle. I'm outside with the kids now. Hey, you two calm down. I mean it!"

What on earth was going on? Darci wondered.

"Don't you know enough to raise your son not to hit a girl?" he demanded.

"No way!" she said. "There's obviously been a misunderstanding."

"I sure hope so. I got out here too late to witness much. Can you come over?"

"Of course." Darci ended the call and parked her car.

"Oh, Christopher. What have you done now?"

CHAPTER SIX

DARCI HURRIED DOWN the street, her high heels clicking. *Damn!* Of all the times not to be wearing her tennis shoes. She pushed her way through the gate that led to Jordan's backyard, and immediately spotted the commotion in the field.

"Christopher!" Darci power walked toward him, her adrenaline surging. "What on earth is going on?" She took in Michaela's skinned knee and rumpled clothing, Chris's torn jeans and the bay gelding grazing nearby, reins trailing on the ground.

Calm down, she told herself.

"He knocked me down—"

"I did not! She tripped."

"—and tried to break my cell phone."

"—just wanted to erase the video."

"Enough!" Jordan's voice boomed, causing everyone to clamp their mouths shut and rivet their attention on him.

"Are you all right, Michaela?" Darci asked,

reaching out tentatively to touch the girl's shoulder.

The girl's lower lip trembled. Her elbow was scraped, too, and she bent her arm to peer down at it. "Great. That'll look real nice with the tank top I was going to get at the mall." Her big eyes widened at Darci. "I only wanted a picture of the horse," she said. "He got all mad and went crazy on me."

"I did not!" Christopher's green eyes darkened. "She's lying, Mom. Her and Jenny were making fun of me, and they were taking a video to be mean."

"How could taking a video of a beautiful horse be mean?" Jenny piped up.

"Get Dollar right now," Darci said to Chris. "What are you doing dropping the reins like that anyway? He could've wandered out of the field and down the street into traffic!"

"He's ground tied." Defiantly, Chris stared her down.

Darci silently counted to ten. "Ride him straight to Uncle Leon's and wait for me there. And don't sweat that horse up anymore, you hear me?"

"Yeah." He shot the girls another hateful look before turning toward the bay gelding.

"I'm sorry," Darci said to Jordan, wanting to give her son the benefit of the doubt, yet feeling the need to make things right. She couldn't imagine Christopher pushing a girl down and hurting her, but then again, she'd never dreamed he would take a gun to school, either. "I'm sure Chris didn't mean to hurt you, Michaela."

"He did," she said, blue eyes welling again. She leaned on her cane. "Ouch." She brushed gingerly at the dirt and gravel stuck to her skinned knee.

"Let's get that cleaned up," Jordan said, then he turned to Darci. "We'll sort this out later."

"Fine." Darci's face heated, and she walked back through the gate and down the sidewalk with as much dignity as she could muster.

Once home, she kicked off her heels, stripped off her dress, and scrubbed the makeup from her face. In her bra and panties, she flopped down on the bed, staring at the ceiling, and allowed herself five minutes to wallow in self-pity. It was a routine she'd adopted in Northglenn after her world had fallen apart. Every night when she went to bed, she'd wash off the makeup that helped her hide how sad and tired she felt, give herself five minutes to cry, then shake off the mood and do her best to move on.

A tear squeezed from the corner of her eye and she brushed it back angrily.

Things were going to work out here in River's End. She just had to give it time. And, truly,

Chris was not unlike any other teen. Everyone had their problems, and in spite of what he'd done in Northglenn, Darci knew deep down her son was a good kid. He'd been through a lot, with his dad remarrying and having twins with his new wife. Not that she was making excuses for Chris. But Ron had seemed to forget his son even existed, outside the monthly court-ordered child support he paid—money Darci put in an account for her son's college education.

If she expected other people to accept Chris despite his past, then she had to do the same. There were bound to be more conflicts in and out of school, just as there were with all kids. She had six more years of him being a teenager, so she'd better be prepared and not overreact every time something happened.

Darci stood and pulled on a pair of jeans. She'd just grabbed a T-shirt out of the closet when a rather loud knock sounded at the door. Trying to turn the shirt right side out, she headed for the living room.

"Coming!" she called.

The knob turned, and the door eased open. Hadn't she locked it?

"Christopher? What are you doing? I—"

Jordan stared at her as she stood there in her bra and jeans, mouth open, holding the lime-green shirt in front of her like a square of origami paper she didn't know what to do with.

He swallowed visibly. "Sorry."

She glared at him. "Are you always in the habit of opening people's doors? I know it's a small town, but…"

"I thought you said come in."

"I said *coming*."

"Right. Sorry," he repeated, belatedly ducking out and closing the door.

Rolling her eyes, Darci slipped the T-shirt over her head, at the same time wondering if she was as red as her bra. "Come in," she said pointedly as she swung the door open.

He stood there for a moment on her porch, looking way too sexy. He stared at her as though she were still wearing only her bra, and now it was Darci's turn to swallow.

Jordan heaved a sigh, as if he found the next words painful. "I had to come and tell you I might've been wrong to blow my stack at Christopher."

"Really?" This wasn't what Darci had expected to hear.

"Yes, really. I overheard Mac and Jenny whispering in the bathroom. I don't think things happened quite the way the girls told us." He looked sheepish for a moment. "I let Michaela know she and I are going to have a talk about it later, when Jenny's gone home. I just thought you'd want to know."

Darci relaxed somewhat. "Thanks. I appreciate it."

"I'll let you know what I find out. See you later." Just like that, he was out the door.

MONDAY AT THE HOSPITAL was busy. It seemed that half the town was there—for surgery, to have babies or with regular emergency fare like fevers and fractures. Darci didn't have a chance to talk to Jordan and see if he'd found out anything more from Michaela.

Tuesday night was the scheduled parent-teacher meetings and open house at River's End Middle School. Darci fixed a quick supper for Chris and her, and they were off. She was about to climb into her car when she spotted Jordan's black Explorer heading their way. He lifted his hand in a wave as he passed.

Four houses apart, and they couldn't ride to a school function together thanks to her kid.

"*They're* going?" Christopher groaned.

"It's not the end of the world," Darci said. "You don't have to talk to Michaela or even go near her."

"Like I would anyway." He shoved his skateboard, which Darci had insisted he bring in case he changed his mind about the park, into the backseat, then climbed into the car.

At the school, Darci found her hands sweating as she looked around, anticipating seeing Jordan in the crowd of parents and kids. Something about him got to her, which was ridiculous. But though she'd seen his car in the parking lot, there was no sign of Jordan or Michaela in the classroom hallways or the cafeteria where the open house was being held.

Darci walked around and mingled with the crowd of parents and teachers. She had a six-forty-five appointment with Chris's homeroom teacher, Mr. Bedford, who turned out to be a tall, soft-spoken man with a firm handshake and a warm smile. His quiet manner switched to one of concern once he and Darci were alone in the classroom.

"Christopher's doing his schoolwork, but just barely," he told her. "It's early days, and he's new here, so he's had a lot of adjusting to do. But I've had to keep on top of him about homework assignments, and he could stand to study harder for tests."

Darci pinched the bridge of her nose. "I was hoping the transition back to a public school from homeschooling would be good for him."

"Oh, I think it will be if we give Chris time and the proper guidance. I'd like to see him make some friends. He pretty much keeps to himself."

"We were just talking about that the other day," Darci said. "Hopefully that's something he'll work on."

She left the meeting minutes later feeling dejected. What had she hoped? To walk into the interview and find out that her son was the Donny Osmond of the seventh grade, all sunshine smiles and happy-go-lucky attitude?

In the cafeteria refreshments were offered, and teachers mingled with parents and students. Darci located Chris, then helped herself to a cookie. She'd just started to take a bite when someone jostled her elbow. Cookie crumbs spilled down the front of her blouse.

"Hi," said a familiar voice.

Darci swallowed the cookie bite and whirled around to look up into Jordan's dark eyes.

"How's your head these days?" he asked.

"All better." She'd practically forgotten about her injury. "We could've carpooled tonight." As soon as she made the statement, Darci had an image of them riding in her car together. Jordan's cologne would fill the vehicle, sending her fantasies into overdrive. Nothing better than a good-looking man who smelled divine.

Bad idea. Why couldn't she stop thinking of him that way?

"I s'pose we could have," Jordan said.

"By the way, I did talk to Chris about what happened Sunday." He'd given her his version of things, and Darci was pretty sure the truth fell somewhere between the girls' accusations and Chris's defense. After all, her son wasn't perfect. He'd made Michaela and Jenny out to be completely at fault, but even if that was the case, Chris had hurt Michaela. And his show-off performance wouldn't have helped matters. "He didn't mean to trip Michaela. She fell over her cane. Still, all three kids were to blame, from what I can gather, and I'm sorry for Chris's part in it. I think he only wanted to show off for the girls, and things got out of hand."

"I'll say," Jordan said. But before she could bristle he held up his hand. "Easy there. I only meant that Michaela had no business egging things on by filming him. And, by the way, I confiscated her cell phone for three weeks. That's if she behaves herself."

"Three weeks, huh?" He'd done well. Darci supposed she ought to punish Christopher for his part, especially hamming it up on Dollar. But he'd been punished enough lately, and his antics had been relatively harmless—at least until he'd yanked Michaela's cell phone out of her hand. Which wouldn't have happened if she hadn't tried to video him… "I told Christopher he should've just ridden away. I don't know why he was that upset over the video. I guess I should ground him for behaving rudely."

Chris had been almost frantic when he talked about Michaela filming him. But by prancing around on Dollar, hadn't he been looking for just that kind of attention?

He'd learned nothing from the negative attention his stunt at Northglenn had gotten, and even after the time he'd served in juvenile detention—or maybe because of it—he'd created minor skirmishes with the neighborhood kids who'd taunted him.

Darci felt dizzy, and it had nothing to do with Jordan's nearness or the lingering effects of her head injury. She was tired of her thoughts running in circles when it came to her son's behavior. She wanted only to move on and give them both the clean start she felt they deserved. Hadn't they paid enough?

"Oh, I see you two are here together." The chipper voice interrupted Darci's thoughts.

She turned to see a tiny woman with spiked blond hair and heels so high, Darci couldn't imagine how she could balance on them. But even the shoes barely put her over five feet tall. Her young face, denim skirt, and colorful sequined T-shirt made her look more like a student than a teacher. Darci had met Shauna Roark briefly when she'd first arrived tonight and knew that she taught classes in both sixth and seventh grades.

"No, actually—" Darci began.

"No, we—" Jordan spoke at the same time.

"Good!" Shauna beamed at them as though neither had said a word. "I have a huge favor to ask the two of you, since you're neighbors and you work together and everything."

"We don't exactly work together," Darci said.

Shauna's forehead furrowed in confusion. "You don't work at the hospital?"

"Well, yes, but—never mind." Darci smiled. "What can I do for you?"

"The annual Sadie Hawkins dance is coming up a week from Friday, and we need chaperones. How about it, you two?"

Darci wanted to refuse, but how could she? She mustered a smile. "I'd be happy to help out."

"Wonderful!"

"I'll have to see what my schedule's like at the hospital," Jordan said.

"Of course. Just let me know." Shauna waved a hand bedecked in rings, purple bangle bracelets and red nail polish. "Toodles." And with that, she was off, balancing on the heels as expertly as a jester on stilts.

"She seems nice," Darci said, feeling a bit awkward.

"She is," Jordan said. "And one of the most upbeat people I know, especially considering what she's been through."

"Oh?"

"Her eight-year-old daughter had a heart transplant about six months ago."

"Oh, my gosh." Darci couldn't imagine going through something like that. It made her own problems pale in comparison. "Is she doing all right?"

"Seems to be. Her cardiologist is a friend of mine. She's in good hands."

Before she could reply, Darci spotted one of Chris's teachers heading her way, a frightened look on her face.

What now?

Belatedly, Darci realized that she'd lost track of Christopher. The last time she'd seen him, he was heading out the door with his skateboard.

The teacher, Rebecca Thompson, looked relieved when she spotted Jordan. "Dr. Drake, thank God. Come quick! Darci, it's Christopher." Her face was pale beneath the cafeteria lights. "Some boys jumped him at the skate park. He's hurt pretty bad."

Darci's heart leapt to her throat. "What happened? I thought the park was being supervised."

"It is. But we can't watch every child every second and, well, it happened so quickly."

Darci was already running out the rear exit, toward the back of the school.

She didn't stop to see if Jordan was behind her, but she could hear his cowboy boots thumping along the walkway, and within moments, he had passed her and was striding down the grassy hillside, taking a shortcut to the park.

Darci followed him, a thousand worst-case scenarios running through her mind. She couldn't shake the teacher's words. *He's hurt pretty bad.*

Dear God, please let Christopher be all right. Please...

She hit the grassy hill running, nearly catapulting herself into a somersault.

By the time she neared the sidewalk surrounding the skate park, she'd spotted the crowd of people but couldn't see Christopher.

"Let me through!" Jordan demanded, way ahead of her. "I'm a doctor."

The crowd parted, and Darci raced ahead to follow Jordan, her gaze frantically searching for her son.

When she saw him, she nearly fainted for the second time in her life. Christopher sat on the ground, between the sidewalk and one of the cement bowls, looking dazed and confused. The top of his head was split open and bleeding, and a large gash streaked his right cheek in a bloody smear. His cap was gone, his hair disheveled… his shirt torn.

"Oh, my God, Christopher!" Darci was at his side in an instant, kneeling on the grass.

"Let me examine him." Jordan spoke firmly, stilling her with a hand on her arm. "I need some room. Did somebody call an ambulance?"

Several people spoke up, confirming they'd dialed 911.

Darci pressed her fingers to her lips, tears burning her eyes. "Who did this to you?"

"Just some guys, Mom," Christopher said. "I'm okay." He spat blood onto the ground beside him.

Then he threw up and slumped sideways onto the grass.

CHAPTER SEVEN

THE INSTANT CHRISTOPHER passed out, Jordan realized the boy's injuries might be more extensive than he'd first thought. While children with head injuries often vomited once, the loss of consciousness could be a sign of more serious head trauma. Carefully, Jordan rolled the boy's head, neck and body as one unit, positioning him on his side to prevent choking in case he threw up again.

Taking care not to apply unnecessary pressure in case the kid had a skull fracture, Jordan gently placed his clean handkerchief against the gash on top of the boy's head.

The ambulance and paramedics arrived in minutes, just after Christopher regained consciousness, and Jordan rode with them to the hospital, instructing Darci to meet him there. She'd lost all color in her face, and he only hoped she wouldn't black out herself. Jordan had just come off shift before the open house, leaving Dr. Samuels on duty. But at the hospital he couldn't see the E.R. physician anywhere.

"Is Dr. Samuels with another patient?" he asked one of the nurses.

She nodded. "We had a traffic accident out on the highway. He's tied up in exam rooms one and two, and Dr. Cheung is still on his way in."

"Give me two minutes." Jordan went to the linen cabinet and grabbed a scrub shirt, ducking into exam room four. He peeled off his T-shirt and threw on the scrubs, then washed up.

With gloved hands, he examined Christopher, who'd been brought into the adjoining room. He lay in a semireclining position on an exam table. Darci hovered nearby. "Is he okay?"

"I'm fine, Mom," Chris insisted. "Other than a splitting headache."

Jordan shined a pen light into the kid's eyes. "That's good," he said, as the pupils responded normally. "What day is it, Chris?"

"Tuesday."

"Who's the president?"

"Obama. Is this a doctor's exam or a pop quiz?"

At first Jordan thought the boy was being flip, but then he realized Chris was scared, using humor to cover his fear.

"I'm making sure your memory is clear," Jordan said. He tended to Christopher's wounds, first numbing them with lidocaine, then flushing them with sterile water before wiping the edges of each cut with disinfectant. The head wound was a good two inches long, the gash on Chris's cheek not much smaller.

Those boys had done a number on him.

"You're going to need a few stitches," Jordan said. "Then we'll get you to X-ray and make sure there's no damage I'm not seeing."

Through a part in the curtain, he spotted two policemen hovering in the hall just outside. For a moment, his mind went back to another time… another pair of police officers.…

"Is he going to be okay?" Darci's trembling voice brought his attention back where it should be. Looking down at her son, she stroked his forehead.

"Mo-om." Chris brushed her hand aside. "I'm not a baby."

"I think he'll be all right," Jordan said. "We'll know more after the X-rays, but he's not showing signs of anything more than a mild concussion." For a moment, Jordan let himself relate to Darci on a level of parent to parent.

Like him, she was a single parent, and Jordan definitely knew that wasn't an easy job. Obviously, she loved Christopher just as Jordan loved Michaela. Still, he couldn't help but be a bit wary of the boy after what had happened the other day, and given his behavior at his previous school. But at the moment, he seemed like an ordinary kid.

"You must have a hard head," Jordan said.

"That's what my mom's always telling me." Christopher glanced at the officers.

"Chris, who did this to you?" Darci asked again. "The police are going to want to know."

"I don't know, Mom. Just some guys, like I told you." He grimaced. "Can we talk about this later?"

Jordan disposed of the used needle in the hazardous-waste receptacle. "That local anesthetic will act pretty quickly. Then we'll get you stitched up. You know, Christopher, all along I've been thinking you look familiar to me."

"I should," Chris quipped. "I'm your neighbor."

Jordan chuckled. "Yeah, all right. But seriously—I think I stitched you up before, when you were younger. Maybe three or four years ago?"

Chris nodded. "My hand and arm." He held up his right hand to display a faint scar. "Uncle Leon's mare threw me into some barbed wire."

"Looks like you got a pretty cool scar to show for it," Jordan said. "And you're going to have a couple more. You and your mom are quite a

pair for banging up your heads." He smiled at
Darci, hoping to ease her tension.

She blushed and smiled back. Jordan continued to talk to the boy as he stitched him up,
wanting to take the kid's mind off the discom-
fort. Darci had stepped out into the hallway to
talk with the officers, and by the time she came
back, Jordan had just finished stitching both
wounds. He pulled off his gloves.

"All set. Now let's get you down to X-ray." An
orderly came and wheeled the boy away.

Darci hung back. "Thank you."

"My job," Jordan said. "No thanks necessary."

"He's really okay?" Worry lined her pale
face.

"Like I said, we'll know more once I see the
X-rays. Try not to worry."

Darci suddenly burst into tears, sobbing quietly
into her hands. "I've never been so—so scared.
Why would those boys do this to him?"

Why indeed? Whatever Chris had done in the
past, he didn't deserve a beating, especially one
that may have been unprovoked, from Rebecca
Thompson's description.

Impulsively, Jordan took Darci by the shoulders, and she crumpled against him. He fought
the sudden impulse to stroke her hair. Her va-
nilla-scented cologne assailed his senses.

Where was his professionalism? Doctors couldn't go around hugging their patients.

"Everything will be okay, Darci. I really believe your son's going to be all right."

Jordan gently extracted her from his arms and handed her a tissue.

"Thanks."

A short time later, Chris was brought back from radiology. Jordan put the films up on the light board and went over them carefully. "Everything looks fine," he said. "But you'll want to watch him closely tonight. Don't let him go to sleep for a while, and wake him up every two to three hours and ask him a simple question like, what's your name?"

"I *know* my name," Christopher said in an exaggerated tone.

"Christopher!" Darci said. "Dr. Drake's only trying to help you." She turned back to Jordan. "Anything else?"

"When you bathe or shower, Chris, be careful not to get those stitches wet for a few days. You can have your family doctor take them out in about ten days to two weeks."

"We don't have a family doctor yet," Darci told him.

"I'd be glad to give you a referral," Jordan said. "Or you can bring him back here to the E.R. Meanwhile, if you see any signs of redness or further swelling, bring him in right away. Or if you notice he shows any signs of confusion or lethargy…excessive drowsiness, that kind of thing. You can give him some Tylenol, but no aspirin or ibuprofen. We don't want to increase the risk of bleeding."

"Thank you," Darci said again. She gave Chris a gentle nudge.

"Yeah, thanks." He dropped his gaze, once more the sulking boy Jordan had seen the other day.

"Can we give you a ride back to the school?" Darci asked.

Jordan had nearly forgotten he'd come by ambulance to the hospital.

"Uh—no, thanks. I've got a couple of things to do before I go. I'll catch a ride with someone."

"What about Michaela?"

"Jenny's mom will keep an eye on her. I called her on my cell."

"Okay then. See you later."

Jordan let out his breath. He'd wanted to accept her offer of a ride, but when he was around Darci he reacted in ways that made him slightly uncomfortable.

For the near future he needed to focus on his career and raising his daughter, not on his good-looking neighbor.

DARCI DROVE IN SILENCE for a few minutes, a thousand thoughts racing through her head. Witnesses had given the police the names of the two boys who'd jumped Chris at the skate park. How could this have happened right under the nose of the teachers, aides and parents who'd been supervising? Darci felt a wave of guilt, remembering she'd been the one to insist Christopher go to the park in the first place.

She'd only wanted him to have fun.

"The police caught the boys who did this," Darci said.

Chris snapped his head around to look at her, then winced. "Ouch." He put a hand to the stitches on his head—six of them. Another four in his cheek. "How did they know who it was?"

His tone told her Chris had known the names of the boys all along. Had he been afraid of ratting them out? Or had he simply not wanted to be known as a snitch?

"Witnesses at the park. Chris, you should've told me."

He folded his arms across his chest. His black-tipped hair tumbled in his eyes, and Darci made a mental note to get him a new baseball cap, even if funds were tight.

"Great, now they're gonna think I narced."

"You don't have to be afraid of them."

"Who says I'm scared?" he asked defiantly. "I don't want to be called a narc, that's all." But his eyes told her different, and Darci wasn't sure which was worse—her son being cyberbullied in Northglenn, or physically bullied here in River's End.

"We're going to press charges."

"Mo-om. No! You can't."

"Chris, we have to. We can't let them get away with this. They're only going to pick on you more if you don't stand up to them."

"Yeah, well I stood up to those creeps at North Star, and look where that got me."

"There's a right way and a wrong way to stand up to someone," Darci said.

"Well, pressing charges isn't going to help," he said.

Was her son right? Was she only going to get him hurt again? She hoped not. But she couldn't sit back and do nothing.

Once home, Chris changed into the boxers he slept in, and crawled into bed to watch a movie on the small TV Darci had bought on sale two Christmases ago. It had been another of the things her son had earned back recently for good behavior.

Exhausted and knowing she'd be up half the night worrying over and waking up Christopher, Darci poured herself a glass of red wine—a rare indulgence—and settled into a hot bubble bath with a paperback novel. But after reading the same paragraph four times without comprehension, she set the book aside and simply sank up to her neck in the fragrant suds, closing her eyes.

Immediately, she recalled the way Jordan's chest had felt when she'd sobbed in his arms. Hard and strong…warm and way too inviting. It had been far too long since a man had held her, and Darci hated to admit she'd liked the feeling.

She thought about the way Jordan had treated Christopher in the E.R. Gone was the defensive father who'd thought Chris had hurt his daughter. Darci liked this softer side of him as he joked with Christopher and tended to his injuries.

And she'd liked the gentleness of the man who'd tried to reassure her everything was going to be all right.

Darci only wished she could be so sure herself.

Willing herself to stop thinking thoughts that couldn't possibly do her any good, she sipped her wine, and told herself tomorrow would be a better day.

CHRIS INSISTED HE WAS well enough to go to school the next day. "I'm not an invalid, Mom. It's just a couple of cuts."

Darci gave in, knowing she did tend to baby him too much at times, and also because she really couldn't afford to stay home from work and didn't want to impose on Aunt Stella and Uncle Leon to keep an eye on him when they had work of their own to do.

Every time she thought Chris was making progress, something seemed to happen. Not that the incident at the skate park was his fault. Darci wanted to give him the benefit of the doubt and allow him to earn the privilege to stay home by himself, even though a part of her was having a hard time letting go.

It wasn't easy watching her little boy grow up and away from her. She told herself he wasn't really going anywhere—he'd likely become closer to her again once he got older and realized that liking your mom didn't mean you were a baby.

By three o'clock, Darci's shift at the hospital was over, and she drove home long enough to change her clothes before heading out to the Shadow S to work.

"Christopher feeling okay?" Stella asked right away. She and Leon had rushed over late last night to see him. Stella had fussed over his injuries, but Leon had told him to cowboy up, jokingly slugging him in the arm.

Chris had laughed it all off, acting irritated

with Stella for fussing like his mom. "You all need to let me grow up," he'd said. "Like Uncle Leon says, I'm gonna cowboy up."

He'd mock-slugged Leon back, as if it was all a game.

But deep down, Darci had seen the fear in his eyes, and she worried if she'd done the right thing by pressing charges with the police. She'd never forgive herself if those boys got back at Christopher for Darci's own actions, beating him up again.

"I think so," she said in answer to Stella's question, "all things considered. He's riding the bus out here after school."

"Any more word on those boys?"

"I had to fill out a police report down at the station during my lunch break. Chris didn't want me to press charges against them, but I felt I had to. Do you think I did the right thing, Aunt Stella?"

"Abso-friggin'-lutely. You can't let the little creeps get away with something that serious. They could've killed Chris."

Darci shuddered at the thought. "I just don't see why they wanted to hurt him. Christopher said he was minding his own business, getting ready to ride his board and try some tricks in the bowl at the skate park, when they started calling him names, and then jumped him."

"Did he say anything back to them?"

"He did admit he mouthed off a little. But that's still no reason for them to hurt him the way they did."

"I'm not saying it is. I'm just saying Chris needs to learn to control his temper. It's what got him in trouble before."

"True."

Had Chris antagonized the boys more than he was willing to admit? Darci sincerely hoped not.

"Well, anyway, onward bound," Stella said. "You're going to like your first riding student today. She's a very special little girl."

"Oh?"

Stella nodded. "You met Shauna Roark at the school last night? Well, it's her little daughter."

"The girl who had the heart transplant? Jordan told me about her."

"Shauna's only child. Her name is Tara, and you'd never know the kid had anything wrong with her. She doesn't complain, nothing."

"Is it safe for her to ride?" Suddenly, Darci felt more than a little apprehensive. She'd be responsible for the child's safety while Tara was riding at the Shadow S.

"Yep. She's got a release form from her doctor. We don't do anything strenuous as it were with the lessons she's taking. She's just learning the basics. Leon and I gave her a scholarship."

"I didn't know you had those."

"We do in cases like Tara's." Stella haltered Dollar as they talked, then began to brush him down. "Poor kid's medical bills are through the roof. And Shauna living on a teacher's salary and what her husband makes down at the garage. It's the least we could do to help them out. Speaking of which, we're thinking about going a step further."

Darci picked up a curry comb and went over the gelding's coat. "How's that?"

"Jordan's wife, Sandra? She used to donate money for kids in need to take riding lessons."

"She did?"

"Yep. She and your uncle Leon used to say the outside of a horse was good for the inside of a kid—and it's true. For most everyone, not just kids. Anyway, your uncle and I are thinking of starting an annual event here in Sandra's memory. I haven't talked to Jordan yet, to get his take on it. But I can't imagine he would object. We'd do a ranch rodeo to benefit someone in need. To help with hospital bills or whatever. Tara would be our first recipient, with all monies raised going straight to her medical expenses."

"Aunt Stella, what a wonderful idea! How can I help?"

"We'll need all the help we can get organizing the thing. We wanted to talk to Shauna about it first, make sure she understands this is something Leon and I want to do annually, so she doesn't feel like a charity case. Woman's got her pride."

Darci leaned over and gave her aunt a hug. "I think you and Uncle Leon are wonderful for coming up with this. And I think Jordan will be honored."

"Aw, go on." Stella blushed, shrugging off the praise. "We're happy to do it. Anyway, don't say anything to Shauna just yet. I figure I can take her aside and talk to her today while you're giving Tara her lesson."

"Sounds good. But should you wait until you've talked to Jordan?"

Stella shook her head. "If he doesn't want us doing the event in Sandra's memory, then we'll do it on our own using the Shadow S name. Either way, it's something Leon and I have put our minds to."

"Okay. I think it's an awesome idea." Darci tugged on her hat brim. "I'll go get Dollar's tack."

As Darci walked toward the barn her cell phone rang. She looked at the ID, and was surprised to see it was Jordan. Speak of the devil. *A handsome devil.*

"Hello?"

"Hey there," he said. "You busy?"

"Getting ready to give a riding lesson. What's up?"

He paused, then said, "I thought you might need to get away for a little bit, after all you've been through lately."

Darci nearly dropped the phone. Was he asking her out on a date?

"What did you have in mind?"

"I'm off tomorrow and there's something I wanted to talk to you about. Want to meet me after your shift at the hospital and see my boat? We can take it for a little spin if you'd like, or just kick back at the shore and have a Coke while we talk."

Alone. With Jordan. On a boat.

She wasn't sure she trusted herself.

Silly. He asked you for a Coke, not hot sex.

"Sure. I'd love to. Is anything wrong?"

"No. Not really. I-it'll keep till tomorrow."

Now her curiosity was really piqued. "Okay, fine."

"Great. Call me when you get off work and I'll come over and pick you up."

"Actually," Darci said, "I've got a riding lesson after my hospital shift. So it will have to be after that."

"That's fine. I'll be waiting."

Darci closed her phone, wondering what on earth Jordan had to talk to her about that required a trip to his boat.

Maybe he was simply trying to get her alone after all.

One could always hope.

But then, having an afternoon fling with a neighbor and coworker wasn't the best of ideas. Especially since she'd told herself she was through with men after her divorce.

But she couldn't help it if her imagination was working overtime.

CHAPTER EIGHT

A THOUSAND TIMES OVER the next day, Darci fought the urge to simply corner Jordan at the hospital and ask him what he wanted to talk to her about. But then, if it were something simple, he wouldn't have asked her out to the boat where they could be alone, would he?

By Thursday afternoon she was more than ready for her shift to end so she could get out to the Shadow S, do her lesson and go meet Jordan. She'd made arrangements for Christopher to ride the bus out to the ranch, where he could do his homework and help his aunt and uncle until Darci came back to get him.

He got off the school bus and sat on the arena fence, watching Darci instruct a little boy and his mother who were taking riding lessons together. When she had finished, Christopher started good-naturedly harassing her as he helped her untack the horses.

"So, you ready for your date with Dr. Drake?"

"It's not a date," Darci said. "I told you, he just has something he wants to talk about."

"Uh-huh. Whatever you say, Mom."

A short time later, Darci was on her way. Knowing she must smell like a horse—though she'd never found the odor unpleasant—she headed for home and a quick shower. She'd barely finished running a comb through her damp hair when Jordan rang the doorbell. Adding a quick touch of lipstick, Darci frowned at herself in the mirror before hurrying to answer it.

"Hi," she said.

"All set?"

"Yep. Where's Michaela?"

"Louise is keeping an eye on her."

She nodded. "Chris is at the ranch, so I guess that just leaves us." *Duh.* She was more nervous than she'd thought. "And I've got something to talk to you about, as well." Leon and Stella had asked her to go ahead and speak to Jordan on their behalf about their plans for the ranch rodeo.

"Well, then let's go."

The reservoir lay just a couple of miles outside of town, so their drive was short, for which Darci was grateful. She felt somewhat strange riding in the big, black Explorer with Jordan. They reached the lake and he found a parking spot near the boat dock. The sweetly pungent odor of sagebrush greeted Darci as she got out of the SUV. Hillsides of sage and rock surrounded the water on all sides.

You're just having a Coke, Darci kept telling herself. It wasn't a real date, and they weren't even going to be alone. With the recent warm fall weather, there were quite a few people about.

Darci looked out over the reservoir. There were several small fishing boats on the water, most with outboard engines, and a few cabin cruisers. In the distance, away from the fishing boats, a couple of people were water skiing.

"Which one's yours?" Darci asked as they walked toward the dock, where several boats were moored.

"That one." He indicated a sky-blue cabin cruiser with dark blue and white accents. The shiny chrome railing had been polished with obvious care. The boat was modest but beautiful, even though it looked like it might be an older model. It also looked like you could sleep on it. Darci blushed at the enticing possibilities.

Maybe being alone with Jordan really wasn't such a good idea. She began to fantasize about taking the boat out on the water with him, dropping anchor in the middle of the lake, sleeping under the stars. No Christopher...no worries. She and Jordan on the gently rocking boat.

What would that be like? Telling herself she

had no business even thinking that way, Darci said, "Nice. I didn't even realize you had a boat."

"I keep the trailer in the garage," he said, "and the boat docked here. That way I don't have to haul it back and forth."

"Good idea."

"I thought this would be a nice place to relax and talk. So, come on aboard." He gestured with one hand.

"Love to." Darci had always dreamed of owning a boat. And in spite of the activity going on around them, it seemed so peaceful here.

Jordan took hold of her elbow to steady her as they stepped off the dock, and she fought back a shiver.

The boat was immaculate, definitely well used but in good shape. Two seats were located next to the driver's, with four more behind it. "I like it," she said. "Looks like lots of fun."

"Thanks. It's a '98 model. I bought it a few years ago from the original owner. It's been a good boat." Suddenly, he looked sad, and Darci wondered if he was thinking of his wife— maybe of happier times spent here with her and Michaela.

"So, you like to fish?" Darci asked. "Or is this more for pleasure cruising?"

"No, we fish," he said. "I've been taking

Mac out since she was about two years old. We started out fishing from shore, then we had a small motor boat, and now this."

"Well, it's nice," Darci repeated, starting to feel uncomfortable. That crazy fantasy was spinning in her head again. She and Jordan…lying on the deck, looking up at the night sky…maybe doing a little night fishing in the moonlight, and then…

"…see below deck?" Jordan was asking.

"Pardon?" Darci felt herself flush.

"I said, would you like to see below deck? There's a little kitchen, and I've got some snacks and cold drinks."

"Sounds good." But her heart hammered. Did she really want to be below deck with Jordan? He looked oh, so sexy in his faded jeans, ball cap, and black T-shirt.

She watched Jordan's taut backside as he climbed down the couple of steps leading below. That fantasy felt on the verge of becoming oh, so real.

"Watch your head," he said. Then he smiled, and Darci nearly oozed into a puddle at his feet. "I guess you're not tall enough for it to matter."

Suddenly, she felt very small, her five-foot-six standing next to his six-foot…one? Two? And those dimples…Lord help her. She'd noticed them a time or two before—when Jordan kidded around with his coworkers, and whenever he'd smiled at her. But she hadn't fully realized how sexy they looked.

Darci looked around the cabin. "This is cozy," she said.

And it was. There was a small galley complete with sink, stove and refrigerator, and the table looked like it folded down into a bed. Off to one side was a curtained area, the dark blue fabric open far enough to reveal a double bed.

Darci swallowed.

"Mac likes eating and sleeping here," Jordan said. "She thinks it's an adventure."

Not the kind Darci was thinking about.

"So, what can I get for you? Pop? Bottled water?"

Her throat was oh, so dry. "Pop's fine," she said, her voice nearly cracking.

"Are you okay?" Jordan asked, staring hard at her.

"What? No. I'm fine." She suddenly wished she was wearing something other than a tank top that showed the swell of her breasts. It had been unseasonably warm today, and she'd wanted to get a suntan, thinking they'd be sitting above deck.

"You aren't nervous, are you?" he asked,

looking over his shoulder as he opened the small fridge.

"Of course not."

"I promise, I'm a perfect gentleman," he said, holding out two cans of pop. "Coke or Mountain Dew?"

"Mountain Dew, thanks."

"I've got snacks, too." He opened a cupboard and pulled out bags of trail mix and pretzels. "Please—sit down." Jordan slid onto the U-shaped bench seat that surrounded the little table.

Darci sat across from him, popping the top on her soda. She took a grateful swig. "That hits the spot."

He nodded agreement and took a long pull of his own drink. Darci watched his Adam's apple move as he swallowed, then he made a satisfied sound and set the can back down on the table. She found herself running her tongue over her bottom lip, her thoughts going places they definitely shouldn't be.

"How's Christopher?" he asked, jarring her back to the moment. "No problems with his stitches or anything…headaches?"

"No, he's doing okay."

"Did you find out why those boys attacked him?"

"The police are looking into it," she said. "I

only hope Christopher didn't do anything to provoke them."

Jordan tossed back a bite of trail mix. "Either
way, it still wasn't right."

"I agree."

"I heard it was Josh Davis and Darren Stark.
They're not normally violent kids, though they
tend to get in trouble sometimes."

"You know them?"

"I've treated them in the E.R. for sports injuries…seen them around town. Darren's dad
keeps his boat out here at the reservoir."

"I guess you never know."

He shook his head. "I guess not. I'm just surprised that the boys would jump Chris out of
the clear blue."

First Stella, now him. "Are you insinuating
Christopher *did* provoke them?"

"Whoa, don't get all defensive," Jordan said.
"And don't put words in my mouth. I'm just
wondering…"

"What?"

"If they heard about what Christopher did in
Northglenn. Maybe that's what made them pick
on him."

"You know?"

He nodded. "That's what I wanted to talk to
you about. I know rumors can get blown out

of proportion, but I do remember hearing news stories about…well, about what happened."

The pretzels Darci had eaten sat like a lump in the pit of her stomach. Of all the reasons he could have brought her out here, that one hadn't crossed her mind. "So why did you want to talk if you already know what Chris did?"

"Like I said, rumors get out of hand and I wasn't sure if Christopher was the boy on the news or not."

"Well, he was, so I guess you can take me home now." Her cheeks burned. He'd only wanted to pump her for information about her son. And here she'd thought he was interested in her.

She moved to stand, and Jordan laid his hand lightly on her arm. "Sit down, Darci. Please. I didn't bring you here to make you feel uncomfortable. I'm just trying to understand, that's all."

"What's to understand?" Her throat thickened. "No one wants my son around once they find out what he did. Didn't you wonder why someone painted *leave* on our garage door?"

"The thought crossed my mind," he said honestly.

"So I suppose you share the same opinion as the other neighbors."

"I don't know what they think," Jordan said.

"But there are people in town willing to give your son the benefit of the doubt."

"Really? And who would they be?"

"Me for one." She'd sat back down, leaning on the table, and Jordan now traced her forearm lightly with his fingertips, making her suppress a shiver. "What happened, Darci? Tell me."

She took a deep breath. "Chris was being cyberbullied," she said, "by some boys who didn't feel he fit in with their crowd. The popular kids. Things got out of hand and Chris couldn't take being picked on anymore. He found a replica gun that belonged to his dad in the back of my closet and snuck it into his backpack. He took it to school the next day. Threatened the boys and some of their buddies with it, letting them think it was real. He served juvenile jail time because of it." Her voice lowered. "Now will you please take me home?"

"I will if that's what you really want," Jordan said softly.

She stood, and Jordan also got up abruptly, stepping away from the table at the same time as she did. They ended up standing toe to toe.

And then Jordan did something that left Darci sure she was daydreaming.

He took a step closer, brushed his thumb

lightly over her cheek, and said in a quiet tone, "I'm sorry, Darci."

Then he bent and kissed her.

JORDAN HAD NO IDEA WHAT possessed him to suddenly kiss Darci. He had to admit the thought had been in the back of his mind ever since she'd come aboard his boat, but he knew he must be crazy to have actually gone through with something he'd fantasized about.

Still, his fantasies were nothing compared to reality.

Darci smelled like fresh air and sunshine and tasted like sweet soda pop. In his arms, she felt all soft and curvy…all wonderful woman. He had the sudden urge to push her shirt up over her head and lay her down on the nearby bed, loving her until she forgot all about her troubles.

Was she wearing a lacy bra like the red one he'd seen her in at her house? He'd caught a glimpse of a black strap beneath her plum-colored tank. Moaning softly, he deepened the kiss, running his hands down her hips to cup her buttocks and press her against him.

She gasped and broke away, her hands moving to disengage his, leaving him hard and wanting.

Lord, he needed her.

Darci looked up at him, her blue eyes wide,

expressive, and for one moment, he saw the longing there, as pure and visible as his own. Then the look was gone, replaced by one of apprehension and…regret?

Aw, hell, please don't let her regret the kiss. Because he sure as thunder didn't.

When she pressed her fingers to her mouth, he wasn't sure if she was hoping to get rid of the memory of his kiss or if she was savoring it.

"That shouldn't have happened," she said.

He'd be damned if he'd apologize. "Why not?" he challenged. "I'm a man, you're a woman, and we're both consenting adults."

"I thought you said you were a perfect gentleman."

Ouch.

"I wasn't planning to tear off your clothes," he retorted, ignoring the inner voice that reminded him he'd daydreamed about doing exactly that. "It was just a kiss, Darci." He stepped back, dropping his hands to his sides. "And I am sorry I upset you. I just needed to know what happened with Chris."

"Because we live down the street from you?"

"Well, frankly, yes."

"And because my son goes to your daughter's school and you were worried he might take an actual gun there and shoot up the place?"

"You're putting words in my mouth again. Darci, I'm just trying to understand."

"Why?"

"What do you mean, why? Because I like you. And Chris seems like a nice kid. I needed to know what would make a nice boy do something like that."

"And now you do."

"Yes, I do. Is there any way I can help?"

Her look of surprise told him it was the last thing she'd expected him to say. But as a physician, as a father, he was used to fixing things.

"Chris is in counseling with your sister," she said.

"I thought as much. Nina's good at her job. I'm sure he'll benefit from talking with her."

"I think so, too." Darci nervously took a sip of her drink.

"You said you had something you wanted to talk to me about, as well?" He indicated their seats at the table. "Sit down, Darci. Please."

She hesitated a moment, then sat. "It's about Sandra."

He clenched his jaw. Did she think that because he'd asked about her son she could now pepper him with questions about the shooting? Was he being unfair not to tell her? After all, she hadn't hesitated to talk to him about Chris.

"What about her?" He couldn't stop the defensive growl that surfaced in his tone.

"It's not what you're thinking. Jordan, my aunt and uncle want to do something to honor Sandra's memory."

He relaxed. "I'm listening."

"You know she made sure deserving kids had the means to take horseback riding lessons at the Shadow S."

He smiled. "She was the kindest, most giving person I know."

Darci smiled, too. "I wish I could've met her. I know Aunt Stella was very fond of her. And that's part of why she wants to put on a charity event in Sandra's name. She and Uncle Leon want people to know how generous she was and they also want to continue that generosity by helping out people in need, especially children."

She went on to tell him about Tara's riding lessons and the rodeo Stella and Leon wanted to hold to raise money to help cover the little girl's medical expenses. "It will be a lot of fun," she said, "and for a good cause. So what do you think?"

He took her hand in both of his and kissed the back of it. "I think it's a wonderful idea. Sandra would be proud to have her name associated with something like that."

"Great." She smiled, visibly more relaxed. "I'll tell my aunt and uncle you approve."

Jordan brushed his thumb across her knuckles before releasing Darci's hand.

She finished her drink. "Well, I guess I'd better be getting back to the ranch."

"No problem. I'm ready."

He was more than ready, and glad they hadn't taken the boat out after all. He was also glad that Darci had brought up Sandra's name. What had he been thinking? True, he'd wanted a quiet place to talk to Darci about Chris, away from Mac and the hospital gossip mill. But a part of him had brought Darci out here because he found the boat and the water romantic, and he found Darci more than a little attractive.

But she had her own life and her own problems, and he had his. He now realized that he didn't have time for a relationship.

He didn't want or need another woman in his life.

There was no replacing Sandra, and that was that.

CHAPTER NINE

CHRISTOPHER PLODDED through the hallway at school, headed for his locker. It had been a week now since he'd been jumped, and the novelty of his injuries was wearing off. At first he'd liked the way people had stared at him in the hall-ways—like they didn't want to cross him. The left side of his face was still pretty bruised, and the stitches on his cheek made him look tough—as if he'd been in a fight that he'd won.

Only he hadn't won. Josh Davis and Darren Stark had kicked his ass, though they'd done it in a chickenshit way. He'd been minding his own business at the park that night, boarding near the bowl he'd been wanting to try—ready to drop down into it—when they'd called him a faggot and a few choice other names. They'd brought up Northglenn, and Chris had lost it. He'd popped back with choice words of his own, and that's when they'd jumped him. Josh had hit him across the cheek with a fistful of rings, and Darren had clocked him in the head with the edge of his skateboard.

Assholes.

He wanted so badly to get back at them, but he'd learned a hard lesson in Northglenn.

"Hi, Chris."

Christopher glanced up from shoving books onto the shelf of his locker, startled out of his daydream by a girl's voice. Kelly Parker stood beside him, her brown eyes staring straight into his. Her long, sandy hair was in some sort of braid at the back of her head. It made her look cute. Pieces of her hair floated all around her face, causing his heart to do funny things.

He liked her almost as much as he liked Jenny, in spite of what Jenny had done.

"Hey," he said, palms going all sweaty.

"The Sadie Hawkins dance is coming up," Kelly said. "I was wondering if you'd go with me?"

She bit her lip, and Chris wondered if she was as nervous as he felt right now.

Say something cool.

"I dunno. Maybe. I mean, yeah, sure. That'd be all right."

Her pretty face broke into a smile. "Cool. I'll call you. Have you got a cell?"

He shook his head. "I broke it," he lied. "Fell out of my pocket when I was grinding some rails on my board."

"Oh, okay. You in the book?"

"Um, I don't think so. We just moved here."
Duh. "I mean, I don't think they've printed our
phone number yet or anything."

"So, can I have it?" She laughed, but she
wasn't laughing at him. The sound was soft and
sweet, and he liked her already, though he barely
knew her.

"Sure, yeah." Chris rattled off the number,
and Kelly punched it into her cell phone.

He wished he *did* have a phone. His mom had
taken his away after all the trouble.

"Right on," Kelly said. "See you later."

She turned, her braid flipping over her shoulder, and walked away. She looked so hot in her
low-rider jeans and the pink T-shirt that showed
off her belly button. He couldn't believe her
folks let her have that little rhinestone piercing.
He was pretty sure she was thirteen, like him.
His mom had had a fit when he'd wanted to
pierce his ear. She'd finally let him, but had put
her foot down when he'd asked to do his lip and
eyebrow.

Couldn't she understand he just wanted to fit
in?

Hard to believe Kelly Parker had asked him
to the dance. And he'd been so lame when he'd
answered.

Oh, well. She didn't seem to mind.

The bell rang, and Christopher looked around the empty hallway. He pumped his fist in the air.

Yes!

He had a date, and that was all that mattered.

DARCI LEANED AGAINST the bathroom sink, looking in the mirror as she applied a cluster of dark brown freckles to her cheek with an eyebrow pencil. She hadn't counted on having to dress up when Shauna Roark roped her into chaperoning the Sadie Hawkins dance. She should've realized if the kids were dressing up...

Minutes later, finished with her makeup and false eyelashes, she surveyed her reflection in the full-length mirror on her closet door. She'd managed to throw together a costume—a polka-dot blouse she'd found at the thrift store, her cowboy hat, and an old pair of cutoffs that were of a respectable length. Coupled with her cowboy boots, the outfit made a passable Sadie Hawkins getup.

"You ready, Chris?"

Darci turned and found him leaning in the doorway, dressed in his boots and some faded jeans and a flannel shirt she'd also gotten at the thrift store. She'd fashioned him a belt out of a piece of clothesline rope, and he'd borrowed a hat from Uncle Leon.

"This is ridiculous." He scowled down at his outfit.

"You don't have to go," Darci teased. "You can always call Kelly and tell her you changed your mind."

"No way." His scowl deepened. "Mom, do you *have* to take us to the dance? Can't you at least drop us off a couple blocks from school and let us walk the rest of the way?"

She hesitated, fighting the protective instinct that rose whenever she thought of the way Chris had been jumped by those boys. She looked at the scarring on his cheek, which Jordan had said would fade with time, and wanted to pull her son into a protective shell.

"Sure, honey," she said, fighting the urge. "That I can do."

His face broke into a smile, and Darci caught a glimpse of her son the way he used to be. Kelly Parker was obviously good for him, though Darci hated to admit her little boy was going on his first date.

"Thanks, Mom. Now can we go?"

She grabbed the hobo bag she'd thrown her lipstick and eyebrow pencil into for touch ups, made sure her car keys were there and headed outside with Chris.

No sooner had she hit the driveway when Jordan's black Ford Explorer came into view. She wanted to hide. But that was silly. She'd seen him at the hospital off and on this past week after the kiss they'd shared, though she'd managed to avoid more than a word or two of conversation. But he'd been corralled into chaperoning this dance along with her. There was no point in trying to avoid him tonight.

Which was a good thing, since he was slowing down and pulling up at the foot of her driveway.

JORDAN TURNED INTO DARCI'S drive on the spur of the moment. Since he already felt like a fool in the hillbilly getup he wore, he figured he might as well be an even bigger one and offer Darci and Christopher a ride to the dance. Why not? Darci and he were both chaperoning, and it seemed silly for them to take separate cars.

Besides, he'd already set up the two rows of passenger seats. Michaela hadn't wanted to go to the dance unless Jenny went with her, since neither girl had a date, and Mac had also invited her aunt Nina to ride with them. A couple more people hardly mattered.

Not just any people, his inner voice reminded. This was the woman he'd kissed and her son, a boy who'd threatened his classmates. He was trying to see Christopher in a more objective light but it was hard. And he kept thinking of ways he could help. But it wasn't his job, he reminded himself.

So why did he keep feeling a need to reach out to the kid?

Jordan rolled down his window, letting in the near-chilly evening air. "Hi, there. Want a ride? I'm going your way," he added unnecessarily.

Darci hesitated, car keys in hand. "Thanks, but—uh—Chris has a date."

Beside her Christopher squirmed, his body language making it plain he wasn't thrilled with his mother's revelation. Jordan managed a half smile at the boy, then focused on Darci.

Simple cutoffs had never looked so good. And they weren't even Daisy Duke-short. "You sure? I'd be happy to pick up your friend, too, Christopher. Might as well save your mom's gas."

Christopher lifted a shoulder, but said nothing.

"We've got plenty of room," Jordan added.

"Sure, thanks," Darci said. "Come on, Chris."

Christopher slouched as he headed for the side door, and in the seat beside Jordan, Michaela shot him an exasperated look.

"Dad," she said, barely above a whisper. "I don't want to ride with *him*."

"It's just a short drive," he said in a low voice. "It's the neighborly thing to do."

Jordan got out and opened the passenger door directly behind his own seat, giving Darci a hand up. Chris had gone around to the other side. "Is this okay?" Jordan asked Darci, "or do you want to swap seats with Michaela?"

"No, this is fine," she said, sliding in and fastening her seat belt.

Jordan tried not to let his gaze linger on her bare legs, but looking higher was just as problematic. The short-sleeved, polka dot blouse showed off her perfect cleavage.

"I like your outfit," she said.

He started, worried she'd caught him staring. "Yours, too. But I feel ridiculous." Jordan tugged at the brim of the straw cowboy hat he wore, then glanced down at his torn jeans—an old pair he normally wore to do yard work or fish in—and the red-and-white checkerboard shirt he'd found at a yard sale.

"Makes two of us," Darci said. But her blue eyes twinkled, and she looked anything but foolish.

Jordan closed the truck door and climbed behind the wheel. "We're picking up my sister, Nina, too, and Mac's friend Jenny. You don't mind?"

"Of course not. The more the merrier." She

gave him directions to Kelly Parker's house—
the girl who was Chris's date. Jordan had treated
Kelly before. He supposed he'd treated more
than half the kids in the county at one time or
another, and a good share of the adult population, as well.

A short time later they arrived at the school
with Nina, Jenny and Kelly. Christopher had
wanted to get out with Kelly a few blocks earlier, but Darci had reprimanded him, telling him
to not be rude. From the look Chris shot her,
Jordan took it she'd broken a promise.

Oh, well.

It seemed strange to hear all four of the SUV's
doors close as everybody piled out. The sound
somehow made Jordan feel comforted and sad
at the same time.

And it reminded him of his promise not to get
too close to Darci.

*Are you watching us, Sandra? Are you glad
the SUV isn't empty tonight?*

Did she know that no one could ever replace
her—that Darci was just a neighbor?

A neighbor you kissed.

"This should be fun," Nina said as they neared
the entrance to the gym. "Thanks for inviting
me, Mac."

"You're welcome, Aunt Nina."

Mac sounded a bit possessive. Was she truly

upset that he'd chosen to share their family evening with Darci and Chris? But Jenny and Kelly were along, too, and Nina as an extra chaperone.

The gym was packed. Shauna greeted them from the table where she was taking tickets. "These double as raffle tickets," she said, stamping their hands. "Thanks again for helping out, you two. And you, Nina."

"Glad to," Jordan said, though he was anything but. While he was always willing to take part in Michaela's activities, he sure didn't relish the thought of sashaying round the gym floor in this getup. At least his cowboy boots felt familiar.

"Well, have fun," Shauna said, giving Darci a knowing wink.

Jordan squirmed. He hadn't thought about the fact that arriving with Darci and her son made it look like they'd come as a couple. *Oh, brother.* Just what the gossip mill needed.

Bales of straw lined the gym's perimeter, offering places to sit in addition to folding chairs. Balloons and crepe-paper decorations covered the walls and ceiling, and a refreshment table was set up at one end.

"You want something to drink?" Jordan asked, desperate for something to do other than ask her to dance.

"Sure," Darci said.

"Sis?"

Nina shook her head. "I'll get my own. I want to observe these kids. Pick their brains a little. It'll help me with my practice."

Christopher had disappeared with Kelly the minute they'd entered the gym, and Michaela had wandered off with Jenny. "Be right back," Jordan said to Darci. He went to the snack table and returned with two Cokes and two bags of cheese curls.

"I love these things," Darci said, closing her eyes in guilty pleasure. "Though I know I shouldn't eat them."

"Yeah, ditto," Jordan said. "Guess maybe we ought to call a meeting of the dance committee and suggest they serve yogurt cups and carrot sticks next year."

Darci chuckled, and Jordan enjoyed the way the sound made his blood tingle. "Somehow I doubt that would fly."

"Probably not. Guess we'd better patrol the dance floor." Jordan made a gentlemanly bow to indicate Darci should go ahead of him, then proceeded to make his way around the gym. Other parents, as well as teachers, mingled with the kids, keeping an eye on everyone. From a raised stage, a DJ spun CDs, keeping the theme country and bluegrass.

"Would you like to dance?" Jordan asked Darci, telling himself this was the perfect way to keep the evening light. He'd already determined their kiss had been a mistake, but there was no reason they couldn't be friends.

"Don't mind if I do," Darci said in good-spirited fun. She gave a little hippity-hop, pony step. "Yee-haw, cowboy. Let 'er rip."

The dance was a brisk Western swing, something Jordan hadn't done in a long time. But he also hadn't forgotten how, and though he felt awkward at first, he quickly found himself falling into step, twirling Darci around the gym's polished floor. The janitor would have some scuff marks to buff out on Monday.

The song ended, and before Jordan could swing Darci back toward the folding chairs, his sister, who'd been dancing with one of the male teachers, spoke in his ear. "Nothing doing, big bro. Take her on a slow one." She gave him a wink, then grinned at Darci. "Don't let him step on your toes, hon."

Darci laughed, and again Jordan fought the curl of nerves in his stomach. This might be a school dance, but he was far from a teenager, so no need to act like one. He cleared his throat and gave her a tip of his straw cowboy hat. "Ma'am," he said formally.

She held out her hand to him once more,

and he took it, pulling her into an embrace that wasn't too intimate, especially given the fact that kids danced all around them. He eyeballed the room until he'd located Michaela. She was sitting on the far side with Jenny, not dancing, even to the slow song. Suddenly Jordan felt bad for his daughter.

She didn't have a date, and with her cane, he knew she didn't really want or expect to dance. She'd only come to be with Jenny and have a little fun with her buddy. He had a feeling Jenny had purposely not asked a boy to Sadie Hawkins just so Michaela wouldn't feel left out.

"Go on and dance with your daughter," Darci said, following his gaze. "After all, I'd say she's the prettiest girl in the room." She flashed him a smile.

He wasn't entirely sure about that.

"I don't know if Mac would want to," he said honestly. He remembered the way she used to dance on his feet when she was small. He'd held her little hands, high stepping so their feet lifted up off the ground in an exaggerated motion. She'd loved it, shrieking and giggling.

Another one, Daddy!

Somehow he doubted that routine would fly these days.

"It's a slow one," Darci reminded gently. "I'l bet she can manage."

"Of course she can," he snapped, then felt bad at Darci's startled look. "Sorry. I guess I'm a little overprotective of her at times. But you're right. Are you sure you don't mind my cutting out on you?"

"Don't be silly." She waved him away, and Jordan hurried over to his daughter's side before the song ended.

"Hey kiddo, wanna dance with your ol' dad?"

He'd thought she would refuse. Instead, a grin spread over her face, and she flashed a smile at him. "See, I told you," she said to Jenny. She handed her cane off to her friend, and leaning on Jordan, followed his gentle lead out into the middle of the room.

"Told her what?" Jordan asked as they danced.

"Nothing." Michaela shrugged. "Just that you weren't really on a date with Darci Taylor."

So she'd been watching him.

"Nope, not a date. Just a friendly dance."

"You didn't finish it."

"That's because I realized I'd rather dance with my daughter," he said.

She beamed at him. Then she sobered. "Dad, do we have to give them a ride home, too? I wanted Jenny to spend the night and she doesn't like Chris either."

"That would be rude, Mac. You know that."

She made a tsk sound. "They can't get a ride with someone else?"

"Probably, but we brought them, so we'll take them home, too. Okay?"

"O-kay. So, can Jenny spend the night? Please? We want to go on the boat."

Last weekend she had decided at the last minute that she preferred to stay home. *Kids.*

"Sure, why not." The song ended.

"Thanks, Dad. You're the best."

"Ah, flattery."

He led her back to where Jenny waited, feeling relieved. He went back on shift tomorrow. Keeping busy with the girls tonight and tomorrow after work would keep him from thinking about how much he was enjoying Darci's company.

"Having fun?" Nina asked as she made her way over. She was dressed in patched jeans, a straw hillbilly hat, and a flannel shirt. "You know, it's good to see you out and about. I was beginning to think you only knew your way to the hospital and back."

"Ha-ha. Yes, I'm having fun, little sister," he said, putting her in a playful headlock. "And you're one to talk. When was the last time you had a date?"

"Men." She waved a hand in dismissal. "Who needs them?"

"Careful there."

"Hey, can I help it if my brother is the only exception to the rule? Find me a good-looking guy with half as many values as you have, and I just might ask him out to dinner." She leaned in and elbowed him in the ribs. "Now, your date's waiting. Go on and dance with her."

"She's not my date. We're co-chaperones."

"Okay. Whatever." Nina grinned then, giving a little finger wave as she walked off to join some women she knew.

Suddenly Jordan was in no mood to dance. He'd given Nina the wrong impression. Had he given the same impression to Darci? Not a smart move, especially after the kiss they'd shared.

Maybe he shouldn't have given her and Christopher a ride after all. He ignored the voice in his head that insisted his motives had been more than neighborly. Turning away from the chairs where Darci was sitting, Jordan walked over to visit with one of Mac's teachers—a guy who enjoyed boating and fishing.

He was soon lost in conversation and nearly forgot he was supposed to be keeping an eye on the kids. He excused himself and walked around the gym, making sure everyone was behaving, and that the unsupervised exits were locked up tight so no one was trying to go out in the parking lot and get into trouble.

At the end of his round, he spotted Nina talking with Darci. He came up just in time to hear them discussing horseback riding.

"Hey, big bro. Darci here tells me she gave you a coupon for a free riding lesson for Michaela. You gonna take her up on it?"

His daughter had been bugging him about that.

"I don't know," he said. "Jenny has horses. If Mac ever learns to ride, she can do it at Jenny's."

That was his excuse. The truth was, he'd kissed Darci and liked it, and he was afraid to see her any more often than he had to.

"Darci's aunt is a professional riding instructor, and so's Darci," Nina continued. "They know what they're doing. Plus Stella's worked with handicapped children before."

"Mac's not exactly handicapped, she's just—" *Just what?* He refused to think of her as physically disabled. "She doesn't need a professional."

"Jenny and her folks are rodeo competitors and all, so they can obviously ride," Nina argued, "but I think Mac would benefit more from lessons with Stella or Darci. You know, it's something she's been wanting to do for a while now. How many times has she bugged you to get her a horse?"

Too many. Michaela had been dragging him to auctions, pointing out that their little bit of acreage was going to waste. She'd nearly had him talked into it before the shooting, then after…

Jordan wanted to throttle his sister for putting him on the spot. "A lot," he conceded.

"Okay then." Nina gestured, palm up. "Let her go riding, Jordan. It'll be good for her. Fresh air, wholesome exercise, professional supervision. What more could you ask for?"

How was he supposed to argue with that?

"I guess. But I want to come, too." He couldn't rest easy knowing his daughter was on a horse and he wasn't there.

"You're more than welcome," Darci said warmly. "We'll put you on a horse, too. Does tomorrow sound good?"

"Tomorrow's fine." He was sure Mac would rather ride than go boating.

Sure enough, Michaela and Jenny had come over just in time to hear the last of the conversation, and Mac let out an ear-piercing squeal, throwing her arms around Jordan's waist.

"Thank you, Dad! I love you more than chocolate!"

He couldn't help but chuckle. "You'd better be careful, missy." He tapped her nose, earning a "Da-ad." "And you have to wear a helmet."

"I'll wear a tutu if you insist, just as long as I

can ride." She and Jenny clasped hands, jumping up and down as much as Mac could manage.

A sudden image of his little girl on a huge quarter horse chilled Jordan to the bone, and he wanted to take back his consent. Tell her she couldn't go after all. But he could hardly do that, given her obvious joy. She hadn't smiled that much in ages.

"We *will* make sure she's safe," Darci said firmly, laying a hand on his arm as Mac and Jenny hurried off to tell their friends.

Fine. But who was going to make sure he was safe from the feelings he was starting to have for Darci?

CHAPTER TEN

SATURDAY MORNING DAWNED slightly on the chilly side, a few scattered clouds threatening to bring showers. Darci hoped the rain would hold off. She wanted today to be perfect for Michaela. She was afraid if they didn't get the little girl's lesson in right away, Jordan might change his mind.

They met at the Shadow S shortly after lunch, and by then the sun had come out, though the breeze was a bit chilly. Darci wore a jean jacket over her T-shirt, and tugged her cowboy hat low over her eyes as she got out of the car with Christopher. Jordan and Michaela pulled in beside them as they were parking, Nina with them.

The girl's entire face lit up like a Christmas tree as she got out of the SUV. "Hi," she said to Darci. "Where's my horse?"

Darci laughed. "Slow down, kiddo. He's not ready yet because I thought you might like to help tack him up."

"I sure would!"

Nina chuckled and Jordan shook his head. "I don't think she slept a wink last night. She was up at the crack of dawn, ready to ride."

"This will be good for her," Nina said. "You'll see."

"I hope so."

"Don't worry," Darci said. "We're putting her on the gentlest horse we have on the place."

"My horse," Chris muttered.

Darci ignored him. "Dollar's great with kids. So come on, Mac. Let's go get him."

Mac leaned on her cane, walking more quickly than Darci had imagined she could. Inwardly, Darci smiled. Nina was right. This was going to be good for the girl.

Darci felt Jordan's closeness as they all walked to the barn with Stella. She still couldn't get the kiss they'd shared off her mind, no matter how many times she tried to convince herself it had meant nothing. If so, then why did it keep her awake at night?

She should just be happy that Jordan hadn't written Chris off as the town villain—that he seemed willing to give her son the benefit of the doubt. She shoved her hands into the pockets of her jacket, not so much to ward off the chilly breeze as to keep from biting her nails. Jordan's nearness had her rattled.

"I saw the flyers for the ranch rodeo," he said. "I take it Shauna Roark approved?"

"She was thrilled," Stella said.

"I'm really glad she didn't have a problem with us doing this for Tara," Darci added. "Hopefully the Indian summer we've been having will come back for a while." The rodeo was planned for the second Saturday in October.

"So, tell me," Nina said. "How does a ranch rodeo differ from a plain old rodeo?"

"The events are a little different," Darci said, "and local ranches compete with each other in teams of four to five people. There will be events like team penning and wild cow milking."

Jordan chuckled. "That ought to be interesting."

"It's something to watch all right," Darci said. "I'll be entering on Aunt Stella's team. It will be her and Uncle Leon, and me and Christopher." She laughed. "I may end up visiting you in the E.R. again."

"We'll hope not," Jordan said, his eyes sparkling.

"How do you milk a wild cow?" Michaela wondered.

"Very carefully," Stella said. "Like Darci said, it's something to behold."

"Can we go, Dad?"

"Wouldn't miss it," Jordan said. It was in Sandra's memory, after all.

By now they'd reached the barn and Dollar's stall. Darci haltered the bay gelding and let Mac lead him out. Jordan looked apprehensive. "Isn't that the horse Chris was riding last week? The one Mac said did all those fancy sliding stops?"

"He won't give you any trouble," Darci said. "I promise. Mac, when you finish riding today, I'll teach you all about brushing your horse down, cleaning his hooves—things like that. Part of the lessons here at the Shadow S are caring for horses, not just riding them."

"Cool!" Michaela said, holding her cane in one hand, Dollar's lead rope in the other. The bay gelding walked calmly at her side, and the girl looked thrilled.

"So, what am I supposed to do while you give her a lesson?" Chris asked. He shot Michaela a resentful glare, and Darci flushed with embarrassment. Michaela was riding Chris's favorite horse, but that didn't excuse his rudeness.

"Why don't you take me on a trail ride?" Nina asked. "That is, if it's all right with your mom and your aunt?"

For a moment, Darci thought she saw Michaela flash her own look of resentment at Christopher. Suddenly Darci knew she needed to trust her son more. "Fine by me," she said. "Aunt Stella?"

"Don't see why not," Stella said. "I'll go with you. I don't get a whole lot of chances to just ride for pleasure these days."

"How am I supposed to ride when she's got my horse?" Christopher asked, again glaring at Michaela.

"Mac has a name," Darci said, "and quit being rude, Christopher. Dollar's not your horse. Besides, you can ride one of the others."

"How about that sorrel Appaloosa we got at the auction?" Stella asked. "I think you'll like him."

"You'd trust me with him?" Chris asked. "I thought you said he was spirited."

"He is," Stella said, "but he's not mean. Okay by you, Darci?"

"Just be careful, Chris," she said.

While Christopher went with Nina and Stella to catch and saddle the Appaloosa, Darci showed Michaela how to brush Dollar down and the proper way to saddle him. Soon they were in the arena, Michaela mounted on the bay gelding. She practically glowed with excitement.

"Look, Dad! I'm riding!"

"I see that." Jordan chuckled from his perch on the arena fence.

Darci noted the look of pride on his face,

even though it was mixed with apprehension. He held Michaela's cane for her, and his knuckles gleamed white.

"Don't worry," she called out to him. "We're good." Then to Michaela, "Okay, sweetie. Hold the reins right about here. You're going to signal him with your legs, through your body language and through the bridle reins." She continued giving instructions, and while Mac had some weakness in her bad hip, she balanced herself in the saddle better than Darci had expected. "Don't be afraid to use the saddle horn," Darci instructed. "There's nothing wrong with holding on any way you can. We'll work on finesse later."

The normal lesson time ran a good hour, but Darci wondered if that would be too much for Michaela's first time. She decided to stop after forty-five minutes. Mac did well, and by the end of the lesson she looked tired but happy.

She swung down off the gelding's back with Darci's assistance. Jordan had walked over, holding his daughter's cane. "You did great, snicker-doodle," he said. "I'm proud of you."

"Thanks, Dad. Can I help unsaddle him, too?" she asked Darci, stroking the horse's neck.

"Absolutely. Like I said, we're going to show you the ropes all the way." She let Michaela lead Dollar to the hitching post, where Darci demonstrated how to untie the cinch, then lifted the saddle from his back and showed Mac how to brush him down. Dollar hadn't worked up much of a sweat, but was slightly damp under his saddle blanket. Once he'd been brushed dry, Darci picked his hooves out, explaining to Michaela why it was an important thing to do, especially after a trail ride.

"A stone caught in his frog or inside the edge of his horseshoe can leave an ugly bruise. It can cause a horse to walk tender footed for days."

Michaela took it all in, wide-eyed.

When they were finished, Darci slipped the hoof pick into the grooming tray along with the currycomb and brushes. "Now I think we'll reward Dollar by turning him out into the paddock with the other horses so he can kick up his heels a little."

"Can I do it?" Michaela asked eagerly.

"I don't see why not." Darci pointed out the paddock, a short distance away. "Just put him in there and take his halter off. Do you think you can manage?"

She nodded. "I can do it."

She took the lead rope, and cane in hand, walked Dollar toward the pipe-rail enclosure.

"Look at her," Jordan said with pride. "I don't know when I've seen her so happy."

"She did really well," Darci said. "I mean that. She's a natural."

"She's always loved horses. Thank you for doing this for her, Darci. I'm sorry I was so stubborn about it."

"No problem. You were just worried. I'm glad she had fun."

Minutes later Michaela rejoined them, and the three of them talked about the upcoming ranch rodeo. "I can take some flyers to school if you like," she said. "And ask permission to hang them."

"That would be great," Darci said. "I—" She broke off midthought as Dollar and several other horses ran across the grass near the barn. Jake barked a warning.

"Oh, no," Michaela said, alarmed. "I must not have gotten the gate latched right. Darci, I'm sorry."

"It's my fault," Darci said. "I should've gone with you."

"Can I help?" Jordan asked.

"We'll need halters and buckets of grain," Darci said. Uncle Leon was out repairing fence, so it was just the three of them. "Don't worry, Michaela. They won't go far."

At least she hoped not.

JORDAN TOOK A HALTER and lead rope and a bucket of grain from Darci. "Stay right here," he instructed Michaela as they headed out of the barn. He indicated a bench seat outside the stables. "Sit there and wait for me, Mac."

"Can't I help?"

"No. Just wait." He felt bad to be short with her, but they had to hurry, and her cane would hamper her movements.

Dollar and the black mare Darci's aunt and uncle had bought at the auction trotted down the driveway as Jordan watched, a paint horse and a buckskin with them.

"I'm sorry," Jordan said once they were out of earshot of Michaela.

"It's okay," Darci said. "Things happen. Next time I'll go with her and make sure she understands how to latch the gate properly."

"If there's a next time," Jordan said.

Darci flashed him a look. "Surely you're not going to punish Mac for this by not letting her take lessons after all?"

"We came to try it out," Jordan said. "I never made her any promises."

"Jordan, that's not fair," Darci said. "I mean, she's your daughter and it's really none of my business how you discipline her, but don't you think you're being a little harsh?"

"I'm not trying to be harsh," he said, walking quickly but calmly toward the wayward horses.

"I'm just being sensible. Mac's not cut out to handle horses."

"Because she left a gate open? Come on, Jordan. It could happen to anyone. You're not using it as an excuse, are you? Because letting Mac on a horse scares you?"

Jordan had to admit Darci's comment held a grain of truth. "I'll think about it," he said gruffly.

"Didn't you see the way she lit up on that horse?" Darci asked. "I thought she was going to burst with happiness."

"I know." He sighed.

"Admit it. Mac was happier today than she's been in a long time. Am I right?"

Briefly, Jordan squeezed his eyes shut. *Sandra...why did you have to leave us?*

"You're right," he said quietly. "That's the happiest I've seen her in ages."

"So, don't take that from her."

"I'm not an ogre," he said. "I'm just trying to look out for what's best for Mac."

Darci laid her hand on his arm. "I know you are," she said. "So am I."

His breath caught. That Darci would feel protective of his daughter left him feeling warm inside. He'd done everything he could since the shooting to take care of Mac and be sure she was safe and happy. Still, he couldn't help but think she missed out on a lot not having a mother. He'd seen the way she looked at Darci today, eager and adoring. Darci had won her over by letting her handle Dollar, tack up the gelding, brush him...

And not getting mad when Michaela made a mistake. Was his daughter hungry for a woman's influence? Maybe she needed someone like Darci in her life. Nina was good with Michaela, and loved her niece beyond a doubt, but she was busy with her practice. Maybe his daughter needed something more.

"All right," he said. "I'll let her come back for another lesson."

"Good." Darci grinned at him. "Now let's get these horses rounded up before Aunt Stella gets back and sees what a mess I made."

That Darci was willing to take the blame for what had happened also touched Jordan. He slowed his pace and walked calmly toward Dollar, shaking the bucket of grain at the gelding. The bay immediately trotted to Jordan's side, shoving his big head into the bucket. The buckskin followed suit, and within minutes Jordan and Darci had the four horses caught and haltered and were leading them back toward the paddock.

Nina, Stella and Christopher appeared over

the ridge, coming down the trail above the stables.

"What happened?" Stella asked as they neared, pulling up on the reins of the sorrel mare she rode.

"We had a little mishap, that's all," Darci said. "Gate didn't get latched properly."

"Dollar's a bit of an escape artist anyway," Stella said. "You don't latch the gate tight, he'll worry it open with his mouth."

Jordan helped put the horses away, and Darci latched the gate, giving it a firm shake to be sure it was fastened securely. His hand brushed against hers as he handed her the halters and lead ropes, and he felt as if his skin had been touched by fire. If he wasn't mistaken, Darci felt it, too.

"So how about you?" she asked. "Do you ride?"

"A little. It's been a while."

"Would you like to go for a trail ride with me sometime?"

Very much so. "Yeah, I would," he said.

"How about tomorrow?"

"I'll have to see," he said. "I promised Mac I'd take her and Jenny out on the boat this weekend. You could come with us," he added on impulse. The voice in his head told him it wasn't a good idea. Especially after the kiss they'd shared last time. Jordan ignored it. "After all, we never did get the chance to go out on the water the other day."

"No, we didn't," Darci said. "Yeah, I think I'd like that."

"Great. Come on down to the house in the morning, say about ten o'clock? You can bring Christopher, too, of course. We'll have lunch on the boat."

"I appreciate that," Darci said, "but I think he's going to stay here at the ranch for the weekend. He really likes working with my uncle."

"I don't blame him," Jordan said. "It's a nice place." Then, "Have you thought any more about letting Christopher have a puppy? I noticed he hasn't come over to see them and they've got their eyes open now."

Darci gave him a crooked grin. "Are you trying to get back at me for getting your daughter on a horse?"

He chuckled. "No. But I think every boy should have a dog. Chris really seemed to want one."

"He does. But I've discouraged him." Darci sighed. "Okay, fair's fair. You let Michaela ride. I guess I can let Christopher have a puppy."

"Good. Bring him over and he can pick one out. But they won't be weaned for a few weeks yet."

"He'll be over the moon," Darci said.

"Mac was, too, when Chewy wandered into our lives. Dogs are a good thing to teach a child responsibility."

Darci bristled. "Are you insinuating Christopher needs a lesson in being responsible? Because I can assure you he's been through the wringer on that one."

"Whoa." Jordan held up his hand. "Not at all. I'm just saying dogs, like horses, are good for kids."

"You're right," Darci said. "Sorry I snapped at you." She hung the halters on a hook inside the tack room. "I'll let Christopher know he can come pick one out."

"PICK OUT WHAT?" Christopher had just stepped into the barn in time to catch Darci's comment.

"A puppy," she said, then laughed as her son jumped into the air, pumping his fist in victory.

"Yes! When, Mom? Now?"

"I don't know. Whenever it's a good time for Jordan."

"You can come now," he said. "Mac and I are heading home anyway."

"All right!" Christopher did a victory dance, and from the corner of her eye, Darci saw

Michaela, who'd been petting one of the horses, give him a dark look.

"We'll finish up here," Darci said, "then I'll run Chris over to look at the puppies. He has to pack a few things to come back here anyway."

"All right. We'll see you in a few. Michaela, what do you say?"

The girl brightened. "Thank you for the riding lesson, Darci. Mrs. Sanders. I had a lot of fun."

"Call me Stella," Darci's aunt said. "And I'm glad you had a good time. I hope your dad will bring you back."

Michaela looked questioningly at Jordan, and he gave her a crooked grin. "Yes. We'll be back." He reached into his pocket and pulled out a checkbook. "I'd like to reserve Michaela a spot for riding lessons."

Now it was his daughter's turn to be excited.

"That's not necessary," Stella said. "You can pay at the time of the lessons. I'll get the sign-up sheet." She ducked into the stable office and returned carrying a clipboard. She conferred with Jordan, the two consulted a calendar, and a short time later Michaela was signed up for lessons.

"Thank you, thank you," she said to her dad and Stella.

"You're welcome," Jordan said. "Now let's get home."

"See you in a little while," Darci said. "Bye, Michaela."

"Bye!"

Darci watched them walk toward the parking area. Jordan's backside was a pleasant sight in his faded Wranglers. *I hate to see him go, but I love to watch him leave.* Darci owned the T-shirt, purchased from a Denver Western store.

Now all she had to do was get the words removed from her heart.

CHAPTER ELEVEN

DARCI WOKE UP THE NEXT morning bright and early. Chris had been so excited after their trip to pick out his puppy. Michaela had possessively clung to one particular puppy she was planning to keep, but Chris hadn't cared. He'd chosen a little blue-speckled male and had already named it Sampson. He'd chatted endlessly with Darci once they'd gotten home, marking off the days on the calendar until the puppy would be old enough to leave its mother. He'd researched pet supplies on the Internet, eager to buy a collar and leash, bowls and chew toys.

Darci had told him to slow down, and reassured him they'd start gathering items gradually—as her budget allowed—from the local pet shop and feed store while they waited for Sampson to be weaned. Chris solemnly promised to take care of the puppy's every need, including house breaking.

Darci only hoped her son would take his responsibility seriously.

Jordan was right. The puppy would be good for Christopher.

In the kitchen now, she fixed a light breakfast of yogurt and peanut butter and honey on toast, then prepared to go out on the boat. She stepped outside in her bathrobe to see what the weather was like. Sunny and fairly warm. Darci showered and dressed in capri pants, a tank top and a light sweater.

As an afterthought, she took a jacket, as well, in case the fickle Indian summer turned chilly again. Tomorrow was the first day of autumn, and she could sense the crispness in the air and smell the leaves beginning to turn.

Her favorite time of year.

A short time later, Darci slipped on her tennis shoes and sunglasses, and walked down the street to Jordan's.

All Michaela could talk about on the ride to the reservoir were the horses at the Shadow S and her riding lesson. "Can Jenny come out to the ranch sometime?" she asked. "She rides really well."

"Of course," Darci said. "You're more than welcome, Jenny," she added, turning in her seat to look at the girl. "Bring your horse if you'd like, and maybe after Mac gets a little more comfortable, you two can ride in the arena together."

"That would be awesome," Mac said.

"Thanks," Jenny added.

Jordan parked in the dirt and gravel lot near the boat dock. He'd brought fishing poles, but Darci shook her head. "I don't have a license yet. Sorry. I'll have to sit this one out."

"It's okay," he joked. "We'll catch 'em, you clean 'em."

"I don't think so," she said, laughing. "I will, however, help eat them. And I'd be glad to cook them."

Now Jordan laughed. "I like a woman who knows her own mind. We can work out something."

On the boat, Jordan made sure everyone was wearing life vests, then headed out into the water. The lake was fairly crowded, and he took them across to the opposite shore.

Darci relished the breeze on her face, and the scent of the water—slightly mossy and fishy, but clean—as they made their way over. Belatedly she realized she hadn't worn any sort of hat or scarf. Her hair would be a mess.

Oh, well.

She was here to have fun, not to win any beauty pageants.

JORDAN STOLE A GLIMPSE at Darci as he steered the boat. She looked gorgeous—a natural beauty—

with her light blond hair blowing in the wind. He only wished her pretty blue eyes weren't covered by sunglasses.

He dropped the fore and aft anchors once they reached their fishing spot, letting them drag and catch before cutting the boat's motor. "Here we are," he said. "This area is a good spot for catching trout and northern pike. Sometimes we even get a few bass. Mac and I come here often."

"All fish look the same to me," Darci said. "Slimy and stinky, but good to eat."

Jordan chuckled. "Well, hopefully we'll catch some dinner today." He helped the girls bait their hooks with salmon eggs, then got his own pole ready and dropped his line into the water.

A couple of hours later, he'd managed to catch three trout. Jenny hooked a bass, and Mac caught a trout and a northern pike. "Way to go," Darci said. "You girls are quite the fisherwomen."

Michaela and Jenny grinned. "I just don't like to take them off the hook," Jenny said, wrinkling her nose. That job had fallen to Jordan.

"I believe," he said, holding the fish up by a stringer, "that someone here offered to cook and help eat these if we caught and cleaned them."

"You got me," Darci said, holding up her hands in surrender. "Looks like I'm your girl."

He wished.

Jordan kicked the wayward thought right

out of his mind. "The galley's all yours then," he said.

Darci baked the trout in the oven, wrapping them in aluminum foil along with chopped onions, bacon slices, lemon wedges and sweet basil. It took only a fork to flake the fish off the bones in juicy bites.

Jordan had cooked fried potatoes and onions and fresh green beans with dill to go along with the trout.

"Man, that's good," he said, savoring a bite of fish.

"Your potatoes and green beans are pretty tasty, too," Darci said.

The girls cleaned up the galley afterward, chattering away about horses. Jordan poured iced tea for himself and Darci, and they carried their drinks up top to enjoy the view from the deck. The afternoon sun was slanting across the water, and the breeze had all but disappeared, leaving the day warm enough.

Jordan stood with Darci at the boat's rail, looking out over the water. "It's been a lovely day," she said. "I had a lot of fun."

"Even if you didn't get to fish?"

"Hey, I got to eat, and that's half the fun right there."

"Only half, though. You'll have to get a license and come out with us again."

What was he doing making plans with her for a future outing? He wasn't even sure if this one had been wise. Jordan couldn't deny the attraction he felt toward Darci, but his heart still belonged to Sandra. It probably wasn't fair to keep seeing Darci without being up front with her about his feelings.

"Darci, I—"

"Jordan—"

"You go first," they said in unison, then laughed.

"I wanted to thank you for inviting me here today," Darci said. "But I can't make a habit of it."

He nearly choked on his tea. Here he'd worried for nothing. "Hey, it's no big deal," he said. "Just two friends having a good time. Enjoying each other's company. Nothing wrong with that, is there?"

Was he trying to convince her, or himself?

Damn, but he wanted to kiss her again.

"What were you going to say?"

"Nothing really. Just something along those same lines. That we need to draw a boundary where our relationship—friendship—is concerned."

He loved the way the sun played off her hair, making it look like liquid white-gold. Loved the way her nose had freckled a bit beneath the sun's rays, since she hadn't worn a hat. And he loved the way her eyes looked without those damned sunglasses. She'd taken them off to eat lunch, but now they were back. Hiding her blue eyes.

"On the other hand, friends can share certain things with one another," he said, stepping closer to her. He set his tea glass down.

"Like what?" she asked. He couldn't see her expression behind the glasses.

"Like a glass of tea, or maybe some wine sometime…or maybe…" he removed her sunglasses, then took the tea from her hand and set it on the table with his own "—a kiss. What's a kiss between friends, Darci?"

Without giving her a chance to answer, or allowing himself to think about what he was doing, Jordan closed the short distance between them and pulled her into his arms. Reminding himself the girls were below deck, he told himself it was only a little kiss he wanted. Just a taste of those luscious lips that had been tantalizing him ever since dinner when she'd licked lemon juice off them while eating her fish.

A kiss between friends…
Who was he kidding?

DARCI SUCKED IN HER BREATH and held it. Surely Jordan wasn't going to kiss her? Not after what he'd just said about maintaining boundaries. But the minute he set down his glass of tea, she knew. And by the time he had her sunglasses off, she was beyond trying to stop him.

She'd tried to tell herself that she wanted only friendship from this man, but the lie wasn't working. She wanted more than that, and had ever since their first kiss. But she couldn't because men couldn't be trusted, not even kind, loving single fathers.

Her own father had left her mother when Darci was only four. She could barely remember him. Then Ron had pulled his stunt, remarrying and becoming the happy-go-lucky father of twins. No, she knew better than to trust a man. And still, she let Jordan kiss her.

He pulled her into his arms, and Darci willingly slipped her own around his neck. She groaned as he parted her lips with his tongue, tracing the line of her mouth. Slowly letting his tongue dip in to taste and tease, then dart out again as he covered her mouth completely with his. She let herself sink fully into the kiss, loving the taste of him. He tasted like sweet basil and lemon, and smelled like sunshine, warmth. He was all husky male.

She could stay like this forever.

"Dad, look at this saddle we found in the catalog—Dad!"

Darci broke off the kiss as abruptly as Jordan

did, her eyes snapping open to see Michaela standing before them on the deck with Jenny, holding a Western tack catalog. Both girls stared wide-eyed at them, Michaela's gaze accusing.

"How could you kiss her?" she shrieked. Then she turned and fled down the steps below deck.

The look she'd given Darci could've melted the anchor and left them all to drift across the reservoir. Darci was pretty sure Michaela would have run much farther than below deck if there had been anywhere else for her to go. Jenny trailed after her, looking embarrassed.

"Oh, God," Darci said. "Jordan, I'm so sorry."

"I'm the one who kissed you," he said, then headed after his daughter.

Darci folded her arms and paced the length of the deck, half contemplating swimming to shore and hitchhiking home.

Jenny came back up on deck, making Darci squirm even more.

"Sorry," she said. "Jordan wanted to talk to Mac."

"No problem," Darci said. "Um. How about showing me that catalog?"

They killed time looking through the book and making small talk while they waited for what felt like forever until Jordan finished his discussion with Michaela. When the two came back up on deck, Michaela wouldn't even look Darci in the eye. She wondered what exactly Jordan had said to his daughter.

"I think it's time we call it a day." Jordan pulled up the anchors and started the boat's engine.

They headed back across the reservoir in silence, and Darci felt sorry that she'd allowed Jordan to kiss her and spoil their good time. Or at least, in Mac's eyes it was spoiled.

Darci hated to admit it, but she had liked Jordan's kiss—maybe a little too much. She was only sorry that it had upset the little girl.

Back at the boat dock, Jordan secured the cabin cruiser, helped Darci and the girls gather their stuff, and loaded everything up into the SUV. He made small talk on the drive home, and Darci helped him out, trying her best to carry on a normal conversation, knowing all the while Michaela was seething in the backseat.

They dropped Darci off at her house, and she thanked Jordan and said goodbye to the girls. Michaela barely mumbled a begrudging goodbye. Darci mouthed "I'm sorry" to Jordan before heading into her house. Inside, she went to the bathroom and splashed cold water on her face, then brushed her hair. The wind had snarled i into a nest of tumbled waves, and she tugged viciously at them, muttering to herself.

"Why, why did you let him kiss you? And why did you have to like it so much?" The last thing she'd wanted to do was hurt Michaela. The death of her mother was no doubt still fresh in Michaela's mind.

Darci changed into jeans, traded her tennis shoes for cowboy boots and put on her hat. She needed to go for a ride to clear her head.

"Looks like you got some sun," Stella said as Darci entered the stables a short time later.

"I went fishing with Jordan. Well, sort of. He and Michaela and Jenny fished. I cooked and ate."

"Sounds like a deal to me."

"You went out on their boat?" Chris asked.

"Yep. Say, Chris, do you mind helping Uncle Leon with the evening chores? I need to talk to Aunt Stella for a minute, and then I'm going to take a short ride before we go home."

"Sure." He shrugged.

Stella waited until he was out of earshot, then sat down on the bench outside the stables. "Sounds serious. What's up, kiddo?"

Darci told her what had happened. "I feel so bad about upsetting Michaela," she finished. "I can tell she's far from ready to have someone stepping into her mother's place."

"She'll get over it," Stella said sensibly. "She's a kid. No kid wants their parent dating someone else. And it's not as if you two are planning on trotting down the aisle anytime soon, are you?"

"Of course not."

"Well, then let her stew. She's not that fragile. I saw what a tough kid she is yesterday. I'm telling you, she'll get over it. Best thing to do is ignore it and act like nothing happened."

"You think? I shouldn't apologize to her?"

"Heck no. What is it with kids today? I mean, I'm sorry for what Mac's been through, I really am. Losing her mother and all that. But in my day, kids weren't the bossy little mini-adults they are today. They didn't rule the roost, the grown-ups did. I think it still ought to be that way, and if you want to kiss Jordan, well, that's your right."

"Wow, remind me to never tick you off."

"Oh, pooh, I'm not that tough. Just practical." Stella gave Darci's knee a firm pat. "Now come on. Get saddled up. You can take the black mare out—I call her Soot—and let me know what you think of her."

"She's not spooky?"

"A bit, but there isn't a mean bone in her body, and she rides like a dream. Got a lope on her to die for."

"All right," Darci said. "I'd love to."

She saddled the black quarter horse they'd bought at the horse auction, speaking soothingly to her as she tacked her up. The mare shied a little when Darci brought up the saddle, stepping sideways, but calmed when Darci soothed her with a word and a touch, lowering the saddle gently onto her back. Soot stood, blinking her eyes in relaxed contentment as Darci cinched the saddle up.

She had a little trouble with the bridle since Soot didn't want to take the bit. The mare was ear shy, too. Guaranteed, some idiot—namely the one who'd abused her—had twitched her ears more than once, a method of controlling a horse that Darci despised. A person would grab the horse's ear and twist it, forcing the horse into submission. It made the animal head shy, and the mare was no exception.

Darci took her time, slipping the headstall on as gently as she could. Once she was in the saddle and headed down the trail, Soot relaxed and eased into a trot and then a gentle lope. Stella was right—the mare's lope was like sitting in a rocking chair. Darci let the mare lope for some distance, then walked her, enjoying the last of the fading sunlight.

By the time she got back to the ranch an hour later, she felt much better, her mind cleared, her body relaxed. Stella was right. Michaela had overreacted to the kiss, and so had Darci. Like Jordan said, what was a kiss between friends?

Uh-huh.

JORDAN FELT LIKE HELL for upsetting his daughter. But at the same time, he wasn't sorry he'd kissed Darci. Now that things were out in the open and he'd been up front with her, he was prepared to simply enjoy her company. And Michaela was going to have to accept that.

September slipped into October without much change in the weather. Jordan knew Darci was grateful for that. The ranch rodeo was coming up, and he couldn't wait to see it happen. He was touched that Darci and her aunt and uncle would want to do something in Sandra's memory. It reminded him to keep things grounded with Darci. He would never forget his devotion to Sandra and no one could ever take her place, no matter how much he enjoyed being with Darci.

As far as the rodeo went, Jordan wanted to help do something other than hand out flyers, but didn't know what.

"What can I do to help?" he asked Darci on a Friday the week before the event.

"Well, we could use someone to run the barbecue. We'll be selling food to help raise money."

"Done," he said. "I am a master of the grill."

She laughed. "Most men are. Or at least think they are."

"Careful," he teased. "You're stepping on my ego here. I am the man when it comes to barbecue."

"All right, all right." Darci held up her hands in mock surrender. "Just so we have some food to feed all those hungry people. Stella and I and some of the ranchers' wives will be making side dishes to go with the meat. Potato salad, beans and all that good ole cowboy fare."

"You're making me hungry," he said. "So, what should I bring to grill?"

"We'll provide all the meat," she said. "It'll be stuff like pulled pork and hot dogs. Maybe some hamburgers."

"Okay. If you need anything else, just let me know."

Somehow, Jordan thought, he had to find a way to have fun with Darci, and still be true to Sandra's memory.

THE DAY OF THE RANCH RODEO dawned clear, but slightly chilly. The events were set to start at ten o'clock. Darci got up bright and early and roused Christopher from bed. He grumbled, but once he was awake, he seemed excited about going.

They arrived at the Shadow S by seven-thirty to help Stella and Leon. By then, the sun was out with the promise of a nice day, and the temperature was gradually warming. Jordan met them at the ranch, and he and Leon set up the barbecue grill and started the batches of pulled pork Stella had made the night before, simmering it on low in cast-iron pans. The aroma of the wood smoke soon filled the air, making Darci's breakfast of fruit and cereal seem like a distant memory.

Contestants from neighboring ranches began arriving a short time later, and soon the place was abuzz, more and more people drifting in as the rodeo drew closer to starting. The portable bleachers quickly filled up with spectators. The rodeo was being held in the arena in front of the stables, and cowboys were busy all around getting the livestock ready. Horses and cattle were run into the holding pens for the bronc riding, the roping events and the wild cow milking.

Trucks and trailers parked everywhere, with roping and barrel-racing horses tied to them. Country music filled the air over the loudspeakers Leon had set up, and from the booth above the arena, Leon and one of the neighboring ranchers, who'd agreed to fill the role of announcer, tested the sound system.

By ten o'clock, things were ready to roll, and the events got underway. Darci hadn't barrel raced in a very long time, and the team barrel racing was something new to her. Each ranch team of four broke into two teams of two, running the cloverleaf barrel-racing pattern side by side, holding a piece of crepe paper between them. If the paper broke, the team was disqualified. The clocked times of the two teams were added, and the fastest combined total would determine the winning team.

Chris had grumbled a bit at running barrels. It was generally a woman's sport in the world of rodeo, though men and boys did compete in barrel racing at gymkhanas. Christopher had run barrels as a kid, and he and Leon had done some practice runs a few days before the rodeo. They would team up together, and Darci and Stella would form the second half of their team. Darci felt a little nervous as she and Stella waited with Chris and Leon at the entry gate for their names to be called.

The guys ran first, turning in a time of just under eighteen seconds. Darci was riding Stella's paint mare, Feather, and Stella rode the buckskin she'd bought at the auction, who'd turned out to be a former gymkhana horse. Together, they entered the arena, and one of the crew handed them a length of orange crepe paper. "Good luck," he said.

"You take the inside," Aunt Stella instructed.

"Feather's got a shorter stride than Buttermilk does."

"Fine by me."

"Keep her in check on the turns until I shout go."

"Will do." Darci nodded.

They took off, flying toward the first barrel. Darci pulled Feather up at the last minute, sliding into the turn with ease. She held her as even with Buttermilk as she could, keeping the mare in check on the turns as Stella took the outside, careful not to tear the crepe paper they held between them. Then they were off as one. By the time they rounded the third and final barrel, the crowd was cheering.

They completed the turn, then took off for the finish line. The crepe paper held, and when Stella let go of it as they crossed the finish line, Darci waved it over her head and let out a victory whoop. They turned in a respectable time of 17.5 seconds, giving them a combined total of 35.4—enough to push the Shadow S into second place.

"Nice ride," Jordan said, meeting them at the gate.

Darci smiled, swinging down off the paint. "Thanks. I didn't think I'd be able to do it."

"And why not? I had every confidence in you."

She laughed. "I'm glad someone did. It's been a long time since I ran barrels." She stroked Feather's neck. "I think I'll take her around for a sip of water." Darci led the mare to the back of the arena where a water trough stood.

"Hi, Darci."

She looked up to see Shauna Roark. She was dressed in jeans, a red-and-purple Western shirt and red cowboy boots. Her blond hair was spiked in its usual fashion, but she'd pulled a purple cowboy hat over most of it. "Hi, Shauna," Darci said. "How are you?"

"Fine, thanks. That was a nice run."

"Thank you. I'm afraid I'm a bit rusty."

"You didn't look rusty to me." Shauna smiled. "I'm having so much fun, and so is Tara. I just can't thank you and your aunt and uncle enough for doing this for us."

"You're more than welcome," Darci said. "We're happy to do it, and I'm having the time of my life."

"Well, good." Shauna looked hesitant. "I hate to spoil your fun, but there's something I wanted to talk to you about, and I didn't think it could wait. I was going to ask you to come into the school to talk to me."

"Oh?" Darci frowned, her stomach tensing. "Is something wrong?"

"It's Christopher," Shauna said. "I've been

having a little trouble with him at school. He's acting out in class a bit, and he's turning in his homework late or not at all."

Darci felt like the wind had been knocked out of her.

"I had no idea. He's been telling me he's getting his homework done. I guess I should've checked it more carefully." Between her two jobs and trying to keep up with the laundry, housekeeping chores and grocery shopping, Darci was exhausted and had readily taken Chris's word that his homework was done. Now she felt like a fool.

"Well, I thought you should know."

"What is he doing to act out?"

"Typical boy things. Showing off in class, talking too much, sometimes talking back to me." Shauna sighed. "Again, I'm really sorry to bring this up here today, Darci, when you and your family have been so wonderful. I don't want to spoil your fun."

"Don't be silly," Darci said. "I'm glad you told me.

"Let me know if there's anything I can do to help," Shauna said. She walked away, teetering on the high heels of her cowboy boots.

Darci let her breath out in a huff. What on earth was it going to take to get through to Christopher?

She didn't know, but one thing was for certain.

They were going to have a long talk once the ranch rodeo was over.

CHAPTER TWELVE

CHRIS FELT A BIT self-conscious as he exited the arena on Dollar. He'd ridden in the team barrel racing and had also been part of the Shadow S's entry in the team doctoring competition, partnering with Leon to do the heading and heeling——roping the steer and holding it—while his mom and Aunt Stella doctored it.

He'd spotted Jenny watching him from the fence nearby and Kelly, too, in the bleachers. He liked Kelly, but he had a huge crush on Jenny, and even though she'd been mean to him, he couldn't stop liking her. She was sitting with Mac on the fence, and he saw them smirk as he rode out of the arena.

Choosing to ignore both girls, Chris rode Dollar toward the water tank and saw his mom talking to Ms. Roark. *Great!* Just what he needed. Were they saying something about him? Telling himself they were probably just discussing the rodeo, since it was being held to benefit Tara Roark, Chris hung back anyway, letting Dollar drink from the stock tank only after his mother had ridden away.

But still, he was nervous. After all, Ms. Roark was his homeroom teacher, and he hadn't been doing so well in school lately. He was dreading the progress reports. But he couldn't help it. He just didn't care about school anymore.

His mom had told him things would get better in River's End. But nothing had changed since he'd left Northglenn, including the fact that he was being cyberbullied again.

He hadn't told his mother, though a part of him wanted to. And he'd finally made a friend at school—Jonathan Baker—who was in his homeroom class. Jonathan liked to skateboard, too, and didn't look down on Chris for riding. He thought horses were "kinda cool."

It was Jonathan who'd pointed out the video clip running on View Tube. It showed him getting his butt kicked by Josh Davis and Darren Stark that night at the skate park behind the school. And if that weren't bad enough, someone had posted anonymous comments on a chatroom page, cutting Chris down, making crappy remarks about what he'd done at his old school. He didn't know who had filmed the video and put it up on the Web site. So many people had been around that night at the skate park, it could have been anyone.

All he knew was he was sick to death of being the butt of everyone's joke.

And thanks to what had happened in Northglenn, there really wasn't a damned thing he could do about it. School sucked, this town sucked and he didn't give a rat's rear about doing his homework.

Still, he knew his mom was bound to find out about his schoolwork sooner or later, and when she did, there'd be hell to pay.

STELLA WAS TICKLED TO PIECES when Darci shared Shauna's gratitude with her. "I'm so glad she's pleased with what we've done," Stella said. "I was afraid of offending her—of hurting her pride."

"Well, you didn't." Darci gave her aunt a hug. "You're one of the most generous people I know, Aunt Stella. You and Uncle Leon, and I think what you've done here is wonderful."

"Oh, go on." Stella blushed. "Couldn't do it without people like you, too, and the other ranch contestants. Even Jordan, helping out with the barbecue." Stella glanced over at Jordan and Leon, who were busy dishing up ribs and pulled pork sandwiches, now that the rodeo events had been halted temporarily in order for everyone to take a lunch break. "But we'll see how you feel about the rodeo after the wild cow milking."

Stella winked.

Darci found a quiet corner outside the arena and tied Feather to the fence, loosening the mare's cinch to let her breathe a little during the break. Then she made her way over to get in line in front of the barbecue grill. She watched Jordan spooning up loose meat onto hamburger buns. True to his word, he looked right at home. He had on a cowboy hat, and a T-shirt that said Kiss the Cook. Darci bit her lower lip, fantasizing about doing just that. She couldn't stop staring at him. Today he didn't look anything like a doctor. Today he was every inch a cowboy. A very good-looking cowboy.

His hair was just visible beneath the black hat, and his espresso-brown eyes appeared even darker than normal beneath the brim. Why hadn't she noticed before how long and thick his lashes were? And as usual, his jeans fit just right, his long legs slender yet muscular. Cowboy boots completed the package in a way Darci found hard to resist.

Jordan looked up and caught her staring, and she felt her face warm. She gave him a little wave, then averted her eyes and continued to wait her turn in line. At last she reached the barbecue grill, plate in hand.

"What'll it be?" Jordan asked, wielding a fork and slotted spoon.

"Make mine a barbecue sandwich," Darci said. "I can't resist pulled pork."

"A sandwich it is," Jordan said. He heaped loose meat onto the bun on Darci's plate. "Want a rib, too?"

"Why not? Pile it on," Darci said. "God, that smells heavenly."

"I told you I was a master griller," he said. "Once you taste this meat, you'll see I didn't lie."

She laughed. "No doubt."

"Don't eat too much," Jordan teased. "You still have to milk a wild cow. Wouldn't want you to be moving too slowly out there in the arena, weighed down by all this good food."

"Very true," Darci said. "Of course, all this food will give me energy, too. That'll be my excuse for making a pig of myself."

"You could never do that," Jordan said, his eyes appreciative, and Darci felt the hair on her neck lift as though someone had tickled it with a warm whisper.

Reluctantly, she moved on, heading over to the tables where local women were serving up potato salad, coleslaw, baked beans and various desserts. Though Jordan had only been teasing her, he had a point. Darci forced herself to take small portions so she wouldn't feel heavy ily weighed down when it came time to ride again.

And he had been right about his barbecuing skills, too. Both the single rib on Darci's plate and the barbecue sandwich were melt-in-your-mouth delicious. "Mmm-mmm, that's better than sex," Darci whispered to Stella. "As if I could remember," she added with a laugh.

Stella nearly choked on her own food. "Lord, girl, what are you trying to do to me! That's way too much information."

Darci laughed, and changed the subject. "Count me in for cleanup duty," she said. "I'll get to it as soon as I finish eating. I can help clear some of this out of the way before the rodeo starts up again and do the heavy stuff after our events are over."

"Sounds good," Stella said. "Thanks again, Darci, for pitching in."

"Of course." She gave her aunt a squeeze.

After the lunch break, the spectators filed back to their places on the bleachers, while the contestants got ready to ride in the upcoming events. Darci retightened Feather's cinch, making sure it was good and secure. Leon would be riding the mare in the wild cow milking, and he sure didn't need his saddle slipping sideways.

Much laughter and joking filled the arena as the announcer declared it time for the wild cow milking. It was one of the wildest, most fun events of the entire rodeo. Leon would be manning the rope—his job to catch and hold the cow—while Darci, Christopher and Stella tried to control the animal long enough to get a small amount of milk into a glass bottle.

Darci readied herself at the starting line with Chris and Stella. At the opposite end of the arena, the big Hereford cross flew out of the roping chute, Uncle Leon and Feather hot on her heels.

The crowd cheered as Leon expertly roped the cow in one quick throw. Next came the tricky part. Stella grabbed hold of the rope, and together with Darci and Chris, she worked her way down the length of it toward the cow's head. The Hereford bellowed and hollered like she was being roasted for lunch while the crowd called out encouragement to the team.

Holding the glass bottle, Darci made her way to the cow's flank. The animal kicked and bucked, thrashing about like a huge fish on a hook. Finally Darci managed to get up underneath her and take hold of a teat. She squeezed, spraying more milk over her hand than she did into the bottle itself. But at last she got enough milk into the bottle to warrant a run back to the finish line.

Just as she turned to make her move, the cow

bucked and twisted beside her. Too late, Darci saw the animal's hindquarters coming her way. She put her free hand out and used her shoulder as well to push the Hereford away. But to her chagrin, the cow pitched high in the air and came down right on Darci's foot.

Red-hot pain shot through the arch of her foot as she stumbled away. She faltered, going down on one knee, but held the bottle aloft in an attempt not to spill the milk. With a shout of triumph, Darci regained her footing and limped to the finish line.

Points were given based on the fastest time and the amount of milk in the bottle at the end of the run. Darci did well on both counts, and the crowd roared. With the help of the arena crew, Leon shook his loop from the cow's head and let the animal go. The Hereford ran bellowing out of the ring, back into the holding pens.

Stella and Christopher raced down to join Darci at the far end of the arena, panting from the exertion of their efforts. "Way to go, Mom!" Christopher said as the announcer called out their time—a respectable one.

"You okay?" Stella asked, out of breath, her brow wrinkled with concern.

"I think so. Ouch." Darci tried to put weight on her left foot but couldn't stand the pain.

Leon had ridden over to them and dismounted

Feather. "Come sit down," he said. "You need to have the paramedics take a look at that."

"It's fine," Darci said. "Just a little sore." But deep down, she had her doubts. She hobbled over to the fence and sat down on the ground outside the arena.

"Let me have a look at that."

Jordan had pushed past the paramedics, who obviously knew him well, and now crouched down beside her. "I thought you weren't supposed to get hurt," he said, teasing her. "Let's see what we've got here." Gently, he took hold of her foot and pulled her boot and sock off.

Darci winced and looked down. Her foot was swollen across the arch, already turning black-and-blue. "Can you move it?" Jordan asked. She did and winced again. Carefully, Jordan manipulated her foot, pressing gently on it. "Looks like a sprain—nothing broken," he said, "but it wouldn't hurt to get it x-rayed, just to be on the safe side."

"I will if it doesn't feel better," Darci said.

He frowned. "You ought to let the paramedics take you to the hospital."

"Jordan, I am not riding in an ambulance. It's not that serious. See." She put weight on the foot, then grimaced again. "It hurts, but I can step on it. I don't think it's broken, either."

"Fine. Will you let me take you, just to be sure?"

"He's right," Stella said, peering at Darci over Jordan's shoulder. Her mouth quirked in a grin, and Darci knew her aunt no more believed her foot was broken than she believed their wild cow could fly.

She was playing matchmaker.

"Best to get it checked out," Leon agreed.

"All right." Darci sighed, knowing it would do no good to keep arguing. Besides, her foot *did* hurt. She supposed there was the chance of a hairline fracture.

"Just let me go check on Mac first," Jordan said. "She's with Jenny." He pointed firmly at Darci. "Sit right there and don't move."

"As if I can," she grumbled. She waited until he was out of earshot and Leon had left to look after his horse. "What are you doing, Aunt Stella?"

Stella raised her brows in an expression of innocence. "Who, me? Why, nothing. I'm just simply making sure you have the best of care from a good-looking doctor." She gave Darci a wink. "What's wrong with that?"

DARCI SETTLED BACK ON the couch with Jordan's help. She felt foolish at all the attention he was giving her. "I'm fine, really," she said. The X-rays had shown no broken bones.

"Well, you've got a sprain anyway, even if nothing's fractured. You need to keep that elevated and put some ice on it. Sit back and I'll get you some from the kitchen."

Darci sat on the sofa and squeezed her eyes shut briefly. *Oh, brother. What had she gotten herself into?* Christopher had stayed behind at the ranch to help Uncle Leon and Aunt Stella with the ranch rodeo and to clean up afterward. Now here Darci was, alone with Jordan, letting him wait on her hand and foot.

He went into the kitchen and came back with some ice in a zip bag, covered by a dish towel. "Come on," he said. "Lean back." He fluffed some pillows behind her and, grateful, Darci eased back onto them. Jordan had taken some extra pillows from her bedroom, and now he put one underneath her leg, gently raising her ankle up and adjusting her foot.

Darci trembled slightly as he touched her. His hands were gentle and confident, and she couldn't help fantasizing how they would feel on other parts of her body.

"There. How's that?" he asked.

"Fine," Darci said. "Thank you."

"Can I get you anything? Something to drink?"

"Don't you have to get back to the Shadow S for Michaela?"

"Jenny's folks are keeping an eye on her. Trust me, she won't miss me. She's having a blast at the rodeo."

"Okay then," Darci said. "Some water would be nice, but you don't have to wait on me. Really."

"No problem. I don't mind at all. Be right back." He took a step away, then turned. "Bottled water or ice water?"

"Either one. There's bottled water in the fridge, or tap water's good, too."

He gave her a wink, then left the room. Moments later he was back with a bottle of water. Darci thanked him, and as she took it from his hand their fingers touched. She looked down at his, noticing how long and slender they were. Jordan rubbed his index finger across her knuckles before letting go of the bottle.

Darci swallowed a gasp.

"That arena dust sure dries a person out," she said after taking a long pull of her drink. "I hadn't realized I was so thirsty."

"Well, I'd say you went above and beyond the call of duty today," he said. He sank down to perch on the edge of the couch. "Doing what you did for little Tara, and in Sandra's memory." His gaze softened. "It means the world to me, and to know you got hurt...well, words simply can't repay you."

Darci swallowed, trying not to notice how good he smelled. "It was no big deal," she stammered. "I'm not the only one who participated in the rodeo, and it was Aunt Stella's idea." Suddenly her throat felt parched, and she took another sip of water.

Jordan reached out and brushed a drop of water from her bottom lip with his thumb. "Yeah, but you're the only one who got hurt," he said.

"I'm glad no one else got hurt," she said. "At least not yet, knock wood. I'm just sorry I let my team down." With Darci out of commission, the Shadow S wouldn't be able to finish participating in the remaining events.

"As long as the rodeo helps Tara, that's all that really matters."

"That's right." Darci smiled.

"I love it when you do that," Jordan said.

"Do what?"

"Smile like you do, when your eyes light up." He leaned closer. "They're so blue. So pretty."

Jordan's closeness left Darci breathless. And his compliment...well, she really didn't know what to do with a compliment from a man.

"I—"

"Shh," he said, hushing her with a soft touch

of his index finger against her lips. "Don't say anything." He scooted even closer, leaned down, and kissed her.

Darci moaned, taking his tongue into her mouth. He made her forget all about her ankle. Everything in the room disappeared except for Jordan. When he wrapped his arms around her, she responded by lacing hers around his neck. She encouraged him to stretch out beside her on the couch. They were alone in the house, and it felt good. They hadn't kissed since that day on the boat.

Darci was tired of sneaking kisses, hoping no one would see. And she was tired of tiptoeing around what she felt for Jordan. She was more than a little attracted to him. She was falling for him, and right now, she couldn't think of anyplace she'd rather be than here in his arms.

Mindful of her sprained ankle, Jordan rubbed his hand up and down the small of her back, locking his mouth over hers. As he deepened the kiss, she sighed contentedly, kissing him back, reaching up to remove the cowboy hat he wore. Wordlessly, she placed it on the end table beside the couch, then did what she'd been longing to do for ages. She raked her fingers through his hair, loving the thick, dark mass of it. Loving the way it felt to her touch.

Jordan kissed her over and over, then pulled

back to peer into her eyes. Softly, he stroked her face, cupping her cheek in his palm. "This is nice," he whispered. "Darci, I can't stop thinking about you. Can't stop wanting to kiss you."

"Then don't," she said.

JORDAN FELT LIKE A MASS of nerves inside. Like a schoolboy. What was he doing? He'd told himself to stay away from Darci, yet that wasn't easy.

"I haven't dated anyone since Sandra died," he told her. "Not really." A couple of dinner dates here and there with some nurses at the hospital, or with a woman a friend tried to fix him up with. Nothing had come of it. His whole focus was on Mac, not his love life.

But Darci was beginning to make him rethink that.

"And I haven't been with anyone since Christopher's father," she said. "I honestly haven't wanted to." She brushed her lips lightly across his. "What are we doing, Jordan?" she whispered.

"I don't know. Just shut up and kiss me some more."

She did.

Jordan folded her all the more snugly into his arms and proceeded to ravish her mouth. Right or wrong, he couldn't stop. Darci felt so good in his arms. So right.

He worked his hands across her back and shoulders, down the front of her blouse. One by one he began to undo the snaps of the Western shirt she wore. And was rewarded with a glimpse of a violet bra, every bit as sexy and lacy as the red one he'd seen her in before. "Aww, Darci."

He sprinkled kisses across her throat, down her chest to her breasts. She moaned as he cupped one soft mound in his hand and kneaded it gently. Then he bent his head and nibbled through the lace of the fancy bra. Taking her nipple in his mouth, he suckled it through the shiny material. Darci mewed with delight, arching her back and lacing her fingers in his hair.

With his teeth, Jordan moved the satin and lace of the bra aside and took her in his mouth. He laved her nipple with his tongue and she let out a sound that was close to a sob. "Jordan," she said. "Please don't stop."

She sat up and, with his help, shrugged out of her shirt. With a flick of his fingers, he had the bra unclasped and slid it from her, looking down at the beautiful curve and swell of her bare breasts. "You're gorgeous," he breathed.

She reached for him, dragging his T-shirt up and over his head. "Fair is fair," she said. She tossed the shirt onto the floor, then placed her palms against his chest and ran them over his bare skin. "Mmm, you feel just like I imagined," she whispered. "Even better."

"How's your ankle?" he asked, half in jest, and half in genuine concern that he might cause her more pain.

"What ankle?" she asked, scooting tight up against the back of the couch, pulling him down to lay beside her. She hooked one leg over his and began to kiss him in earnest once more.

"You feel so good," he said. "You don't know how long I've been wanting to do this."

"Mmm-mmm," she said. "Me, too. But I—I was afraid."

"Afraid? Of what?" He stopped for a moment, looking deep into her eyes.

"I know a lot of people think the worst of me and Christopher, because of what he did. I was afraid you'd be one of them."

He wanted to be honest with her. "I was for a little while. I didn't think I wanted to get involved with you, and not just because of Chris. I felt torn because of Sandra, but I know she'd never want me to stop living. And being with you feels perfect. This day has been perfect." He held her, rubbing his hand over her shoulder. "I see now that Chris is on his way to healing, too. I hope my initial feelings about him were wrong."

"Whoa, wait a minute. Back up." Darci's brow furrowed. "You're hesitant about getting involved with me because of Chris? I thought when we talked about what he did, you said you understood?"

"I do understand, Darci. I just want to be sure everything's right with him. I mean, if you and I are involved, that means he and Michaela will be spending time together. I told you before I know he's in good hands with Nina. And he was having such a good time at the rodeo today. He seems to be doing well. But if there's anything I can do to help fix things with Chris, I want you to tell me."

"Fix things?" She locked her gaze on his. "You want to *fix* my son? Jordan, there's nothing wrong with him. He's had problems in the past, yes. Problems we're still working on. But he doesn't need to be 'fixed.' He's not a broken bone."

"I know that, Darci. You're taking this all wrong."

"Am I?" She shook her head. "Here I thought you were different than everyone else who pre-judged my son. But now I find out you want to *fix* him." She sat up, covering herself with her shirt.

"Darci, please don't be upset. I only want to help."

"We don't need your help," she said, blue eyes sparking. "Like always, we're doing just fine on our own."

Jordan was so intent on repairing the damage he'd done with his careless words that the sound of truck doors slamming didn't immediately register. Darci gasped, pushing off the couch and hobbling over to peek through the curtain.

"Oh, my God! It's Aunt Stella and Christopher! Hurry." Darci gathered her bra along with her shirt and made her way toward the bathroom as quick as she could.

Jordan scrambled to snatch his T-shirt from the floor and shove his head through it. As a last minute thought, he grabbed Darci's water bottle and rushed for the kitchen. He got there just in time to hear the front door open and Christopher call out, "Mom! I'm home."

Quickly Jordan tucked his T-shirt into his pants, raked his fingers through his hair, and stopped to catch his breath. Then, a fresh bottle of water in hand, he came out of the kitchen as though he were simply bringing the water to Darci.

He had a feeling Stella wasn't fooled. For one thing, his hat was sitting on the end table. Then Darci came hobbling out of the bathroom a moment later, her hair freshly combed—except for a little piece sticking up in the back—and her blouse snapped and tucked. But she looked like…well, like she'd been thoroughly kissed.

Or was it just his imagination? His guilty conscience?

"Hi, Stella," he said brightly. "Christopher."

"I thought you were at the rodeo," Darci said, running a hand over her hair.

Stella looked from one of them to the other, and Jordan could see the older woman *knew.*

"We were," she said, "but it's just about over. At any rate, the Shadow S is out of the running, so I thought we'd come check on you and see if you needed anything." She raked Jordan with a knowing gaze. "But I can see you're in good hands."

"I—I'm fine," Darci stammered.

Stella placed her hands on her hips. "Uh-huh. And what are you doing on your feet, Missy? You need to lie back on the couch and *rest.*" She looked sternly at Jordan.

"I, uh, had to go to the bathroom," Darci said.

"Uh-huh," Stella repeated, biting her lip.

"I brought you some water," Jordan added. He gave Darci a smile, and for a moment she looked confused. Then she got it, and smiled back.

"Oh, thanks. I could use some." She sank down on the couch, coughing slightly. "Throat's a bit dry."

She situated herself on the sofa, putting her foot back up on the pillow Jordan had brought her.

"So, how's it feeling, Mom?" Christopher asked, looking down at Darci's foot. "Man, it's turning purple. That ol' cow got you good."

"She sure did," Darci said. She leaned back and gave her aunt a wide-eyed, innocent grin.

"You forgot something," Stella said.

"Oh?" Darci looked puzzled.

"Your ice pack." She picked it up and laid it across the top of Darci's foot. But Jordan saw her do something else as well.

She leaned in and gestured at Darci who looked down.

"Your shirt," Stella whispered.

Jordan took a closer look.

The snaps on Darci's Western blouse were crooked.

CHAPTER THIRTEEN

DARCI'S FOOT REMAINED stiff and sore by the time Monday rolled around. She purchased a cane at the local drugstore to help her maneuver enough to go to work. While her foot couldn't support her complete weight, it was better than on Saturday. She spent the next few days working at the hospital, avoiding Jordan then going home to Christopher. Stella had taken over her riding lessons to give her a chance to rest her foot, especially since she couldn't get her cowboy boot on.

By the end of the week she was back teaching—from the ground in tennis shoes. Gradually her foot felt better, and she was able to put her boot back on, though gingerly.

She'd just come home from the Shadow S on Friday afternoon when the doorbell rang. Darci opened it to find Jordan standing on her doorstep, holding Chris's puppy.

"Hi," he said. "Somebody's ready to come home, if you're ready to have him."

Darci stiffened, but invited him in. She still

hadn't been able to forgive him for what he'd said about wanting to "fix" Christopher. "He's eight weeks today, isn't he?" she asked. "Chris has been counting down on the calendar. I was going to call you later to see if we could come get Sampson."

"Perfect."

"Chris," Darci called. "Someone's here to see you."

"Who?" His voice held a note of curiosity as he came in from the kitchen. The minute he saw the puppy, his entire face lit up. "Sampson! Is he really here to stay?"

"You bet," Jordan said. "Eight weeks old, finally."

Christopher took the puppy and snuggled him, and Sampson responded by nuzzling Chris's neck and licking his face, his tail wagging a mile a minute. "I've got his stuff all ready," Chris said. "A bed, his food bowls, toys…everything."

Jordan laughed. "Well, good. I hope you enjoy him."

"I'll take really good care of him," Chris said. "I promise. Can I take him up to my room, Mom?"

"As long as you watch him so he doesn't have an accident."

"I will. Thanks, Jordan." And with that, he bounded up the stairs.

"I haven't seen much of you at the hospital," Jordan said.

"I've been keeping busy." Darci shifted uncomfortably.

"Are you sure you haven't been avoiding me?"

His words stung, since she knew they were true. "Maybe I have."

"I think we need to talk," he said. "Is there someplace we can go this weekend? I can get Louise to keep an eye on Mac."

Suddenly Darci just wanted to get everything out in the open with him. "How would you like to go for a horseback ride?" she asked. "Chris loves spending time at the ranch with my aunt and uncle, and I have lessons to give tomorrow, so I'd planned to take him out there with me anyway. He can hang around with Uncle Leon while you and I take a ride."

"It's been a while since I've been in the saddle," Jordan said, "but I'd love to go. It sounds like fun. What time?"

"I have lessons in the morning until just after lunch. How about one o'clock? We can pack some sandwiches and eat them out on the trail."

"Sounds good. I'll meet you there. And since you're providing the horses, I'll bring lunch."

"Okay," Darci said. "See you then."

When he left, she closed the door and leaned against it. Her heart was racing. Time alone out on the trails with Jordan. It wasn't exactly what she'd had in mind, but then, it would give them a chance to clear the air with no interruptions.

Darci went upstairs to check on Sampson and Chris. The two were playing with a tug toy, and Darci laughed at the puppy's antics. She was glad she'd let Jordan talk her into the dog. Chris seemed happier than he had been in a long while.

The next morning Darci did her best to focus on her riding students. Ever since she'd upset Michaela by kissing Jordan, Mac hadn't been quite as friendly to her, and she'd been seeing Stella for her lessons. The girl was set to have a riding lesson tomorrow, and Darci had every intention of putting things right with Jordan so that his daughter would feel comfortable with her.

Darci was just leading Feather from the barn when Jordan pulled up in the ranch driveway. He got out of the SUV, wearing his boots and cowboy hat and a Western shirt. Darci tied the horse to the hitching rail, then greeted him. "Hi. You ready to ride?"

"As ready as I'll ever be. You going to put me on that paint?"

He'd seen Feather in action at the ranch rodeo, and he looked dubious.

Darci chuckled. "I don't think so. She might be a little too much horse for you until you get your sea legs back, so to speak. I thought I'd let you ride Dollar."

"That's a relief. I guess if Mac can handle him, I can. Though maybe not," he added as an afterthought, and laughed.

Darci grinned. "You'll be fine. It's like riding a bicycle. Come on. I'll let you lead Dollar from the barn and brush him."

A short time later they had both horses tacked up and ready to go. Jordan handed over the lunches he'd packed, and Darci slipped them into Feather's saddle bags. She found Stella in the barn long enough to tell her where she was headed, and to warn Christopher to behave himself. Then she and Jordan were off.

They took a trail leading from out behind the barn, up over the ridge through the sagebrush. It was one of Darci's favorite places to ride. The route edged groves of aspen and pine then climbed to breathtaking views. Darci let Feather pick her way through the high meadow grass toward a stream that wound through the timber. The water flowed crystal clear over the rocks, like a soothing song.

"I love this trail," she told Jordan. "The sound of the water always calms my nerves."

"I can see why," he said. "It's beautiful here." Dollar plodded along beside Feather.

"There's a small clearing up ahead," Darci said. She often stopped there to rest and meditate. "We can eat our lunch there."

"Sounds good to me."

They rode to the spot and Darci swung down off Feather's back. Jordan did the same with Dollar, walking a bit stiffly. "Guess I am out of practice," he said with a grin.

"You're getting there," Darci said.

They tied the horses to a sturdy tree branch, and Darci unpacked their lunch from the saddle bags. She'd tied a blanket across the cantle of her saddle and spread it out on the ground beside the stream while Jordan laid out their lunch.

"This looks good. Thank you for bringing it."

"No problem." He had packed fried chicken, macaroni salad, grapes and pound cake for dessert. He'd also brought bottled green tea.

Darci sat back on the blanket and bit into a drumstick. "Mmm-mmm. Did you make this?"

"I'm afraid not. It's from the deli."

"I didn't know they had such good chicken." She realized she was making small talk, avoiding what they'd really come here to discuss. But since Jordan had been the one to suggest they talk, Darci decided to let him bring up the subject. She didn't have long to wait.

Jordan served them slices of pound cake once they'd finished the chicken and salad. "Darci, we need to talk because I think we've both been avoiding the issue of what happened last Saturday."

"True," she said. "So what exactly do you want to talk about?"

"That was the closest I've come to making love to a woman in a long time," he said. "I haven't been with anyone since Sandra."

She nearly choked on her cake. *Two years?* The man had gone without sex for two years? And here she thought she'd had a dry run. "It's been a while for me, too," she said.

"I don't take what we did lightly, and I'm sorry I upset you."

"I just wasn't prepared for you to be so judgmental of my son. I thought you were different than other people." A few parents at the Shadow S had refused to let Darci give riding lessons to their kids. Not many, but the rejection still stung.

"I'm not trying to judge him, Darci." Jordan looked directiy into her eyes. "I didn't mean what I said to come out that way. I only want him to get the help he needs, which I know you do, too, and if there's anything I can do, let me know. That's all I meant."

"You said you didn't want him around Michaela."

He shrugged. "Darci, I have to be protective of Mac. She's been through a lot."

"Chris has, too. Maybe not like Mac, but he's had his share of troubles."

"Okay, so we're in agreement that we both want what's good for our kids." It wasn't a question.

"Of course."

"Okay. Then why are we arguing?"

"I don't want to argue with you, Jordan. I just don't want you misjudging Chris."

"I guess I need more time to get to know him." He scooted closer on the blanket. "And to get to know you, too." He reached out and brushed his hand across her face. "I like you a lot, Darci."

She liked him, too. And she wanted to see where things might go between them. But how to do that and guard her son's feelings and best interests at the same time?

"Can't this be about us for the moment?" he asked.

Oh, she wanted that. How she wanted it. She needed something strictly for herself. Everything had been about Christopher for so long now. Darci felt selfish thinking that way, but she couldn't help it.

"What about us?" she asked in a low voice. She felt almost afraid to move, afraid to breathe.

"I'd like to pick up where we left off," he said. He reached up and gently removed her cowboy hat. "Let me kiss you, Darci. I want to taste your lips again." He leaned in and she held her breath.

She should stop him. But she didn't want to. A part of her said this could go nowhere. Things were complicated with the kids, but surely they could work around that. Darci closed her eyes and met Jordan's lips. He kissed her softly, then slid his tongue inside her mouth. With a little moan, she wrapped her arms around his neck, and he laid her back on the blanket, caressing her hair, her face…letting his hands roam down her back.

"Darci. Sweet Darci," he whispered.

His hands found the buttons on her shirt and as she let him undo them, Darci told herself to stop. That this couldn't possibly go anywhere. She didn't trust him not to hurt her, but most of all, she didn't trust him not to hurt Christopher. Ron had done enough damage to their son to last a lifetime. She was sure that was part of Chris's reason for acting out.

And still, she couldn't stop herself from melting in Jordan's embrace. He found the clasp on her bra and with gentle hands undid it, freeing her breasts to his touch. He kissed and caressed her, taking his time, drawing first one nipple into his mouth, then the other. Darci reached for the snaps on Jordan's Western shirt. She undid them and pulled the shirt back over his shoulders as he shrugged out of it.

He was all hard planes of muscle…firm, solid male. Hungrily, she ran her fingers over his shoulders, loving the feel of him. She removed his hat, setting it on the edge of the blanket with her own. Then she lay back and enjoyed the attention he leisurely lavished on her body. At last his hands found the button on her jeans and slipped it open, then reached for her zipper. Darci tensed with anticipation as he tugged the zipper down. He reached inside her jeans, inside the lacy underwear she wore, and she had to bite her lip against a cry of pleasure as his fingers found her most intimate place, already hot and wet with wanting him. He slid his fingers inside her, and she moaned against his mouth.

"Jordan," she said. "I want you."

"Mmm, and I want you, Darci. But I want to take my time with you. Make you feel all the pleasure I can give you."

Darci groaned, then reluctantly pushed him

away. "I didn't come prepared," she said, then blushed when he looked at her curiously. "You know. Protection."

His mouth quirked in a little smile. "I did," he said, reaching for his wallet.

Darci wasn't sure whether to be relieved or offended that he'd been so certain something would happen between them. She decided to go with relieved. Still, she gave him a hard time. "Awfully sure of yourself there, cowboy," she said as he pulled the condom from his wallet.

"Not sure," he said. "Just hopeful."

"That I can live with."

She resumed kissing him, now boldly reaching for the button on Jordan's own jeans. She found him hard and ready for her, and she reached inside his boxer briefs to stroke the length of him, making him moan with pleasure. Soon they lay undressed in each other's arms, and Darci trembled, goose bumps rising along her flesh. It had been far too long since she'd been intimate with a man, and she wanted Jordan in the worst way. Wantonly, she rubbed her bare foot up and down his calf, inviting him to take her.

"Not yet," he said. "I'm not through with you, Darci."

He started with her mouth, nibbling kisses across her lips, then moved to her neck and her throat. He rained kisses and tiny nips across her skin, making Darci squirm. He took his time at her breasts, laving the nipples, tracing the areolas with his tongue.

Then he laced his fingers through hers and raised her hands up above her head. "I want you to lie like this," he said. "And let me make you feel good, Darci. I want to love every inch of you."

She sighed, completely lost. "Be my guest."

JORDAN WANTED NOTHING more than to plunge inside Darci. But giving her pleasure, watching the way her features melted into a mask of sheer ecstasy, made making love to her well worth the wait. The way her eyes had gone all soft and dreamy made him feel good inside. He'd dreamed of making love to her, but nothing had prepared him for the reality of Darci's beautiful body, the softness of her creamy skin.

As he nibbled kisses down her stomach, Jordan took in the scent of Darci's perfume. It was soft and subtle, vanilla and spices, mingling with Darci's own clean, womanly scent as he worked his way down her thighs. Wanting to heighten her pleasure, wanting to tease and tantalize her, he kissed and licked the sensitive area between her thighs. Darci mewled like a kitten, writhing beneath him, wanting more. She laced her hands in his hair, guiding his mouth lower.

Unable to resist her any longer, Jordan plunged his tongue inside her wet warmth. Darci let out a gasp, this time clutching the blanket with both hands. She writhed beneath him as his tongue found the tender nub of her flesh. She tasted as sweet as honeycomb, and Jordan took his time enjoying her, loving the way he made her gasp with pleasure.

And then she plunged over the edge, crying out as an orgasm wracked her body. He watched as she rode one wave after another, eyes closed. Then she blinked and opened them, staring up at him with twin pools of blue.

Jordan sprinkled kisses along her neck as he lay beside her and opened the wrapper on the condom. He slipped it on, then slid inside her in one smooth motion. Nothing had felt so good as her warm, sweet tightness clamped around him. She cried out as he entered her, then ran her hands over his shoulders, pulling him close.

They moved as one, their bodies rocking together in a rhythm as natural as the rippling water of the stream. Jordan reached down and cupped Darci's buttocks, loving the firm feel of them. Her skin was so soft, like peaches. He captured her mouth, kissing her, as he moved his hips against hers. And then he climaxed, throbbing inside her, feeling as though he were going to explode.

He slumped against her, his hands wrapped in her hair. He ran his fingers through the strands of it, then caressed her cheek, sprinkling kisses down the heated skin to her lips. "That was beyond fantastic," he said.

"I think all the bones in my body have melted," Darci said, then yelped as Jordan's mouth found a ticklish spot behind her ear.

"What say we try for round two."

"What about condoms?" Darci peered up at him, biting her lip.

He grinned. "Let's just say I felt a little more sure of myself than I admitted."

He reached once more for his wallet, pulling out a second condom. Darci reached up and pinched him on the butt. "You sly dog."

"Woof."

And with that, he began to love her all over again.

DARCI QUIETLY DRESSED, already feeling regret. While physically she was satiated, emotionally she was sure she'd lost her mind. Nothing could come of making love with Jordan. He'd already admitted that deep down he didn't trust her son. He had to protect his daughter. And she had to protect her son and her heart.

Despite the intimacy they'd shared, she sure couldn't trust Jordan with either one.

Why had she been such a fool to make love with him?

Because she'd needed him. Physically. It was plain and simple as that. He was a man and she was a woman, and they'd come together in need and nothing more.

"You okay?" Jordan asked as they mounted their horses and started back toward the Shadow S.

"Fine," Darci lied. "How's it feel to be back in the saddle?" She felt her face turn hot. "I didn't mean—"

Jordan chuckled, making Darci blush even more. "I know what you meant," he said. "It's fine, Darci."

But it wasn't.

CHAPTER FOURTEEN

"I HAD A GOOD TIME, Darci," Jordan said when they arrived back at the barn. "You can't see scenery like that except on horseback."

"True," she said, relaxing a bit.

"Mom!" Christopher came hurrying over. "Aunt Stella gave a lesson to Shannon Long, one of the girls in my homeroom, and she invited me to her birthday party next Friday. They're having pizza and everything. Can I go? She said Michaela's going," he added, looking at Jordan.

Darci was so pleasantly surprised, she answered without a moment's thought. "Of course. That's great, son." First Jonathan and now Shannon. Maybe Chris was finally starting to make friends. Knowing he would be hanging out with a group of kids that included Michaela did her heart good.

"Yes!" Chris pumped his fist. "I'm going to tell Uncle Leon." He hurried off.

"So, you know the Longs?" Darci asked Jordan.

"I do. They're good people, and Mac already asked me if she could go to the party."

"Great." Darci chewed her bottom lip. "You don't have a problem with her hanging out with Christopher then?"

"I never said your son was a monster. And no, I don't have a problem with them being at the same party."

It wasn't exactly what she'd asked him, but Darci let it go. "Just checking," she said.

Jordan helped her unsaddle the horses and brush them down. Darci kept up idle chit-chat as they worked, regretting more and more that she'd made love to him. When they were finished, she walked with him out to his truck. He moved to kiss her goodbye, but she avoided contact.

"Not here, Jordan," she said in a low voice.

For a moment, he looked hurt. "We're hiding what we shared?" he asked.

What *had* they shared? Sex? Lovemaking? For Darci it had been the latter, though she hated to admit it. She was more drawn to Jordan than she'd ever thought she could be, given their circumstances.

"I think it's best if we forget about what happened, Jordan," she said honestly.

His lips thinned. "I see. Okay. If that's the way you want it. Thanks again, Darci, for taking me horseback riding. I enjoyed it, and I hope we can do it again sometime."

Did his words have a double meaning, or was her imagination simply working overtime? "I'm glad you enjoyed it," she said, deciding to ignore the question. "I'll see you later, Jordan." She stepped back from his vehicle, raising her hand in a wave.

JORDAN DROVE HOME, CONFUSED and out of sorts. What had just happened with Darci? He had no doubt in his mind that she'd enjoyed the lovemaking they'd shared as much as he had. And he truly had enjoyed their horseback ride together. Spending time with Darci was something he could definitely make a habit of. So why was she upset?

He racked his brain, trying to decide if he'd done something wrong—said the wrong thing. But he came up empty. Then it hit him. It was still about Christopher. Had to be. He muttered a curse. Why had he said anything in the first place?

Because he'd wanted to be honest with Darci. He liked Christopher, but he was still leery of him after what the boy had done in Northglenn. Jordan wished he could discuss Chris with Nina, but both of them respected patient confidentiality. So all he had to go on were his own instincts, his gut feelings. And those feelings told him to tread softly when it came to involving Chris in his little girl's life. Being at a party where Chris was—that was one thing. But there was no denying that if he took things further with Darci, Michaela would be spending a lot more time with Christopher.

Maybe it was best to take a step back and think things through. But Darci had wanted to flat-out forget about any kind of relationship. Something he wasn't willing to do.

He'd let down his guard, and already she'd hurt him.

Why, oh why, had he been so quick to make love to her?

DARCI FOCUSED ON WORK for the next week. But it wasn't an easy task to keep Jordan off her mind when she ran into him at the hospital.

Finally Friday rolled around—the day of Shannon Long's birthday party. Chris had been so excited, but he hadn't known what to buy the girl for a birthday present. Darci had taken him shopping after making a discreet phone call to Shannon's mother to get some suggestions. After finding out the girl had pierced ears, Darci had helped Chris pick out some cute earrings and a matching bracelet.

Now while he got ready for the party, Darci

showered and changed from her riding clothes. She wanted to look presentable when she dropped him off at Shannon's house, so she dressed in khaki pants, a cute print blouse and her tennis shoes. Chris put on a good pair of jeans that weren't baggy and a T-shirt. Darci had finally made him an appointment for a haircut, and he looked much better minus the dyed black ends.

Darci ignored Chris's protests as she walked with him to the door of Shannon's house. "I've talked to her mother over the phone," Darci said, "and now I want to meet her in person, Chris. Case closed."

"Fine." He slumped along beside her, walking as though she'd put him on a leash and a choke chain.

A short time later, Darci was back in the car alone. She'd enjoyed talking to Shannon's mother, Vivian, a pleasant woman who looked about her own age. Suddenly, Darci didn't want to go home to an empty house. She didn't know what to do with herself. Aunt Stella and Uncle Leon had plans for supper at a friend's house, so a visit to the ranch was out.

She drove home anyway, and as she passed Jordan's house, she saw him out in the yard, raking leaves in the late afternoon sun. On impulse, she pulled into his driveway and got out of the car.

"Hi. Doing a little yard work?"

He nodded. "This warm weather we've been having isn't going to last forever. I figured I'd take advantage of a nice day and get a little work done." He leaned on the rake. "Are we really going to talk about the weather, Darci?"

She shook her head, and on impulse said, "What are you doing for supper?"

"Nothing special. With Mac at the party, I figured I'd whip up something quick and easy."

"Would you like to eat with me? I mean, since we're both alone with the kids gone?"

His gaze softened. "Sure. I'd like that very much."

"It won't be anything fancy," Darci said. "Let me run to the store, and you can meet me at my place, say in an hour?"

"I'll be there."

JORDAN SHAVED AND SHOWERED, telling himself Darci's dinner invitation wasn't a real date. She was merely being friendly since both their kids were at Shannon's party. Still, he couldn't get their lovemaking out of his mind. Darci's words echoed in his memory.

I think it's best if we forget about what happened.

But he couldn't forget. He'd lain in bed the past few nights, remembering how Darci felt beneath him…how she'd looked, lying on the blanket with no clothes on, her soft hair framing her face, her skin bare to his touch. He wanted more.

He was definitely falling for Darci, no matter what his better judgment told him.

With a bottle of wine in hand, Jordan walked down the street to her house. He wondered if the neighbors were watching, seeing him approach her door with wine in hand. He didn't care. Let them think what they wanted.

Darci answered his knock almost immediately. "Come on in." She held the door wide, and he stepped inside.

"I brought this." Jordan held out the wine.

"Thank you. But I can't drink. I'll be driving later to get Christopher from the party."

"Right." He hadn't been thinking. He had to get Michaela, too. "One glass, maybe?"

"One should be fine," she agreed. "Come on in to the kitchen."

He followed her through the living room into the brightly lit kitchen. Although he'd been there before, he hadn't really noticed how homey the kitchen was. A round pine table that seated four was tucked in a nook beneath the window, a basket of fresh fruit in the center. Green-and-white gingham curtains were tied back at the window, and roosters were everywhere—ceramic knickknacks, salt and pepper shakers and on the dish towels and pot holders hanging near the stove. There was even a charming, whimsical rooster clock hanging on the far wall. The entire room gave off a welcoming, country air.

Jordan peered through the window overlooking the fenced backyard. "How's Sampson doing?" he asked.

"Still crying for his mother now and then, but overall he's fine. Chris already has him spoiled rotten."

"Glad to hear it."

"I hope you like sub sandwiches," Darci said. "Homemade ones, that is." She took the makings for the sandwiches out of the grocery bags on the counter.

"Love them. Anything I can do to help?"

"Pour us a glass of wine, if you'd like." She laughed. "I don't know what color of wine goes with subs. Jordan, I'm sorry I didn't make anything fancier."

He felt foolish, bringing wine. "It's my fault," he said. "The sandwiches are fine, and the wine's a red, which goes with meat, right? So we'll wing it. Do you have a corkscrew?"

She indicated the second in a row of drawers and Jordan rummaged through it. He opened the wine and poured it into two glasses Darci got out of the cupboard.

"Mayonnaise or mustard?" Darci asked.

"Mayo's fine." He watched as Darci made the sandwiches—sliced roast beef on wheat. She put Swiss cheese on them and served them with potato chips, pretzels, pickles and olives. And bottled water in addition to their wine.

"I hope these are okay."

"They look good to me." Jordan bit into his sandwich. "So, why did you invite me here tonight, Darci? Really?"

She swallowed a bite of sandwich. "Maybe because I feel bad about sending you home so abruptly last weekend."

He covered her hand with his. "Don't feel bad," he said. "I understand." Or at least, he was trying to.

They ate together in comfortable silence. "Are you up for a movie?" Darci asked. "A DVD, I mean?"

"Sounds good," he said. But deep down, he wondered how he could spend an entire evening with Darci and not touch her.

DARCI TRIED TO LOSE HERSELF in the romantic comedy she had talked Jordan into watching, struggling not to think about his nearness on the couch or how good he smelled. Images of him lying naked beside her on the bank of the stream last weekend flitted into her mind, making her insides weak. She was beginning to question her sanity in asking him over tonight.

She was so on edge she actually jumped when Jordan's cell phone rang.

"Excuse me," he said, then flipped the phone open. Immediately his expression made Darci think he had an emergency at the hospital. Oh, well. Their evening would have to be cut short after all. Jordan spoke quickly into the phone. "I appreciate the call, Mark. I'll get right over there. Talk to you later."

He closed the phone and faced her. "Darci, that was a paramedic who's a friend of mine. He just went on a call to Shannon Long's house."

All the blood rushed from Darci's head straight to her feet, leaving her feeling disoriented.

"What is it? Who's hurt? Is it Christopher? Michaela?"

"I'm not sure. There was some sort of scuffle." He put his hand on her shoulder. "A gun was involved."

"No." Darci squeezed her eyes shut. This couldn't be happening again. "What gun? What happened?"

Christopher wouldn't...

"Mark wasn't clear on the details. He just wanted to let me know he was on the scene."

Darci switched off the DVD. "Let's go." She ran to her bedroom and got her keys and wallet.

"Can you drive?" Jordan asked.

She wasn't sure. She was shaking so hard. "I don't know."

"Let me." He reached for her keys, and Darci gladly handed them over. Together they hurried outside to her car and took off for the Longs'.

The fifteen-minute drive felt like forever. When they reached the house, a crowd was gathered on the front lawn. Red-and-blue lights from three police cars and an ambulance cast an eerie pall on the scene. "Christopher!" Darci jumped from the car, calling his name, Jordan right on her heels.

Frantically, she scanned the crowd, and then she spotted him, standing near the porch with Michaela. "Chris!" She rushed forward, and for once, he came into her embrace without protest.

"Mom!"

"Daddy!" Michaela said, rushing into Jordan's arms. "I was so scared. S-so scared." She began to sob hysterically. "They had a g-gun."

"It's okay, honey," Jordan said. "I'm here. Who had a gun?"

"I don't know their names. Some older friends of B-Ben's."

"Jenny's brother Ben?" Jordan looked appalled.

Michaela nodded.

"Are you hurt?" He held her at arm's length, and she shook her head.

"No, but I would've been if it weren't for Chris."

"Where are Shannon's parents?" Darci asked, looking around.

"They were upstairs," Chris said. "The party was in the basement, but we'd gone outside for a little while when everything started happening. Mr. and Mrs. Long didn't know what was going on."

"I want to know exactly what *did* happen," Darci said. "Come over here and sit down." She led Chris to a brick wall surrounding a flower bed and sat on the edge of it. Jordan and Michaela sat down, too.

"Start at the beginning," Jordan said.

It was Michaela who spoke first. "I did something awful," she said. "Jenny, too." Her eyes welled with tears. "Jenny and I—we—we were picking on Christopher because he'd been talking trash about us at school."

Chris's face turned red.

"Chris, is that true?" Darci asked.

Looking down, he scuffed the toe of his sneaker against the ground. "I was jealous of her," he said. "Of all the time she's been spending out at the Shadow S with you, and then Aunt Stella. And I was mad that Jenny laughed at me when she found out that I like her. So I started a rumor that Jenny and Mac are easy."

"Chris!" Darci stared at him.

"We wanted to get back at him," Michaela went on. "But we didn't mean for things to go this bad. We said some terrible things about Chris, and we got Shannon to invite him to her party as a prank. We just wanted to get him here and make fun of him in front of everyone because of the way he'd embarrassed us at school."

Before she could go any further, a police officer spotted them and approached. He exchanged greetings with Jordan, then turned to Darci, extending his hand.

"Frank Gibson," he said. "Are you Darci Taylor? Christopher's mother?"

"Yes. Officer, what's going on?" Worry gripped her stomach in a tight knot. "Has Chris done something?"

"Nothing wrong, that's for sure. Let me explain to you what's happened here tonight." He propped a foot up on the brick wall, leaning one elbow on his knee. "Are you familiar with Jenny and Benjamin McAllister?"

Darci nodded. "I've met Jenny—Mac's friend, right? And Ben is her brother."

"What's happened, Frank?" Jordan sounded impatient. "Are Ben and Jenny hurt?"

Officer Gibson pressed his lips into a thin line. "Ben and his buddies are in a lot of trouble. They apparently came here tonight with intentions of hurting your son, Ms. Taylor."

Darci gasped, looking at Chris. "Why?"

"It's my fault," Michaela sobbed. "Mine and Jenny's. That's what I was trying to tell you."

"The girls posted some rumors on the Internet about your son," the officer went on. He shifted uncomfortably. "Some were of a sexual nature."

Darci's jaw dropped.

"Mac?" Jordan looked stricken.

"Jenny and I didn't do that part," Michaela said. "I swear, Dad. We only posted some pictures and a video of Christopher that Jenny got from Ben."

"Pictures of what?" Jordan asked firmly.

Mac hung her head. "Of the night Chris got beat up by Darren and Josh. Some friends of Ben's were there, and they took pictures and videos with their cell phones. Ben forwarded them to Jenny, and we put them online. But we didn't have anything to do with what Ben and his friends said, I swear."

Chris finally spoke up. "They said horrible things."

"I'm sorry, Chris," Michaela sniffed. "I never meant for things to go so far."

Darci sat back, stunned, as the police officer filled in the blanks. Jenny and Michaela had found out about Christopher's crush on Jenny, who'd come up with the idea to post the photos and video of Chris on My Page. "She and Michaela wanted to embarrass him with photos of him 'getting his butt kicked,'" Frank Gibson said.

But it was one of Ben's friends—Daniel Vanguard, an older boy—who had caused the most damage. He'd found out about Christopher's crush on Jenny and had blown things out of proportion.

Daniel had spread a rumor that Chris had asked Jenny to perform oral sex on him. Ben had believed the rumor and been furious, coming instantly to his sister's defense. Ben, Daniel and some boys from Daniel's class had crashed the party. Some of the boys had been drinking, and they'd come to Shannon's house to teach Christopher a lesson.

They'd planned to beat him up, but Daniel had taken things even further. He'd brought a gun, intending to scare Christopher, and it had gone off accidentally. Michaela would have been shot if it weren't for Christopher's quick actions.

"We were teasing Chris," Michaela said, "Jenny and I, when Daniel brought out the g-gun. He fired it, Dad." Her face turned white as she spoke. "It went off right near me, but Chris had already pushed me behind him, back out of the way."

"You did that?" Darci asked.

"I knew how scared she was," Christopher said bravely, even though his voice trembled. "I was pretty scared myself, and—well—I knew what Michaela had been through with her mother and all. I just pushed her behind me without really thinking about it."

"I'm proud of you," Darci said, giving her son a hug.

"I don't know what to say, Christopher," Jordan said. "I can't thank you enough."

"That's not all," the officer said. "We found some rope and duct tape in the trunk of Daniel Vanguard's car."

"Oh, my God." Darci clamped a hand to her chest.

"We think Daniel and his buddies had something pretty bad in mind for Christopher. We're taking statements from everyone right now. We'll know more once all the witnesses are interviewed, and we're going to need statements from you kids," he added, addressing Chris and Mac.

"Can it wait until later, Frank?" Jordan asked. "I think the kids have been through enough for one evening."

"I need a brief statement from both kids tonight," Frank said. "Then I can come by your house tomorrow and we'll finish the paperwork. I'll want to talk to Christopher again, too, Ms. Taylor."

"That's fine." Darci nodded. "Whatever you need."

"I'll get some forms for you to fill out," Frank said. "Be back in a minute." He turned and headed for his patrol car, leaving Darci sitting in shock on the brick wall.

She shook her head. "I don't even know what to say." She felt ashamed that she'd thought the worst of Chris when the paramedic called.

"I don't know how to thank you, Christopher," Jordan repeated. He clamped a hand on her son's shoulder. "If you hadn't acted so quickly..."

Chris shrugged. "I just pushed her behind me."

"Here comes Officer Gibson," Jordan said "Let's get your statements filled out so we can get out of here."

While Christopher spoke with the police officer, Darci made it a point to find Vivian Long and ask her how things had managed to get so out of hand.

Vivian looked extremely contrite. "I am so, so sorry, Darci," she said. "I know you don't really know me, but Jeff and I do our best to supervise Shannon. We didn't mean to be lax in not watching the kids. I never thought twice about letting them go outside. Jeff had started up the barbecue grill, and they were toasting marshmallows. I'd just checked on them before all this craziness happened."

Darci's accusations left her like air from a deflating balloon. "It's not your fault," she said. "Things happen."

Darci knew that only too well.

CHAPTER FIFTEEN

DARCI TALKED TO CHRIS for quite a while once they got home. Her son was visibly shaken, and for once Darci let him put Sampson in bed with him.

"I've never been so scared in all my life, Mom," he said as they sat on the edge of his bed. "And it made me realize something."

"What's that?"

"No matter what I went through in Northglenn, it's nothing compared to what Mac's been through, losing her mom like she did." He shook his head. "I never really understood until that gun went off and I pushed Mac behind me. She got shot before, Mom. And she had to watch her own mother get shot and *die*, right in front of her eyes." He swallowed hard. "I can't even begin to imagine that."

"You're not mad at her and Jenny then? For their part in this?"

He lifted a shoulder. "I was at first. But it seems sort of pointless."

Darci reached out and hugged him. "I know,

son. Michaela's been through the wringer for sure." She brushed his hair back from his forehead. "I'm so proud of you, Chris, for what you did. Mac could've been hurt again if it weren't for you." *Or worse.*

"Mom?"

"Yes?"

"There's something I need to tell you. Something that I should've told you a long time ago."

Darci frowned. "What is it?"

"I want you to know why I did what I did back in Northglenn."

"I understand, sweetie." She took his hand in both of hers. "We've gone through all that, right?"

"But you don't know the real reason," he insisted.

"What are you talking about, Chris?"

"I wasn't just being cyberbullied. One of the kids at school made it look like I was sexting."

"Sexting?" Darci couldn't believe her ears.

Christopher's face reddened. "Yeah, it means—"

"I know what it means, sweetie." Text messaging with sexual content.

"There were some boys in my gym class, and they were picking on me. The same kids who were cyberbullying me. One of them—Troy

Montgomery—started harassing me after we'd showered. I was drying off with a towel, and Troy took my cell phone. Mom, he took a picture of my butt. And then he forwarded it, along with a crude message, to all my friends in my contacts list."

Darci sucked in her breath. "Oh, my God, Christopher! Why didn't you tell me?"

"I was too embarrassed." His voice choked up. "It was awful, Mom. My friends were laughing at me, and Troy sent the shot to his own cell and then forwarded it to his friends, too. Everyone was making fun of me. That's why I took the gun to school."

Darci couldn't have been more stunned. Fury at the humiliation her son had suffered raged through her.

"I don't even know what to say, Chris. I can call the Northglenn police, see about pressing charges."

"No!" He looked horrified. "It's all over, Mom. I just want to forget it. Just like I want to try to forget what happened tonight."

"Okay. If you're sure." Darci wasn't certain she could live with not seeing Troy Montgomery punished. But she didn't want to put Christopher through hell again.

"Did you talk to Nina about this?"

"Not yet. I've been debating."

"I think it's a good idea, Chris. Please think about it."

"Okay. I will."

Darci bent and kissed her son on the forehead. "Try to get some rest now, son. I love you."

"I love you, too, Mom."

Darci made a mental note to get in touch with Nina the next day and see if she could fit Chris in for an appointment. Talking to his counselor would be beneficial after what he had been through tonight.

He'd nearly been shot!

The thought terrified Darci.

And to find out he'd been through more in Northglenn than she'd known about...

In her bathroom, she filled the tub and sank into a hot sea of bubbles. She leaned back, sipping a glass of the wine Jordan had brought over for dinner. How must he feel, after what Michaela had already been through? Darci didn't hold Mac's part in what had happened tonight against the girl. Mac was just a kid who'd made a costly mistake. The same as Christopher had in Northglenn.

Once the bathwater had cooled, Darci slipped into a warm pair of pajamas. The evening air had turned brisk—typical Colorado weather. In October you could be scraping the frost off your windshield in the morning and the bugs off it at night. Darci crawled into bed with a book, determined to try to forget her problems for a little while. She was absorbed in the plot of the romantic suspense when she heard a soft knock at the front door.

Who in the world…?

Throwing back the covers, Darci slipped into her robe and went to see. She turned on the porch light and peered through the curtains at the front window. Jordan stood on her porch.

Quickly, Darci opened the door. "Jordan, what's wrong?"

He gave her a sheepish smile. "Nothing, really." He raked a hand through his dark hair. "I can't sleep. I decided to take a short walk, and I saw your bedroom light on and thought I'd stop." He took a step backward. "I can see you're ready to go to sleep. I'm sorry to have bothered you, Darci."

"Actually, I was just reading," she said. "I couldn't sleep, either." She held the door wider. "Want to come in?"

He hesitated. "I can't leave Mac for long. She's sleeping, and Louise is keeping an eye on her." He stepped inside and gave a short laugh. "Would you believe Louise has a police scanner, and she'd already heard about what happened? She knows the Longs and recognized their address, and she knew Mac was going to

Shannon's birthday party, so she put it all together and came over to see if Michaela was all right. That's when it hit me hard, and I told Louise I needed some air."

Darci motioned toward the couch. "Sit down, Jordan. It'll be okay."

He sat, then looked at her, his expression one of frustration. "I feel like I want to stand over Mac all the time to protect her." He looked straight into Darci's eyes, his own sad and serious. "Darci, how in the world do I protect my daughter?"

JORDAN SAT IN DARCI'S living room, feeling the weight of the world on his shoulders. He'd had to force himself to leave the house minutes ago, and even then he'd taken his cell phone, in case Louise needed to reach him. She'd reassured him she'd be right there in case Mac woke up. And still, it was exactly as he'd said to Darci— all he wanted to do was hover over Michaela.

It was the same way he'd felt after Sandra's shooting.

"Want some wine?" Darci asked.

He nodded. "That actually sounds really good right about now."

She went to the kitchen and came back with the wine bottle and two glasses. She poured them each a glass, nearly finishing off the bottle.

She handed Jordan's to him, and when he took it, he realized that his hands were shaking.

"Are you all right?" Darci asked, sitting beside him on the couch.

He took a sip of the wine. "It didn't hit me until I got Michaela home," he said, "how close she'd come to—to being shot again." He raked a hand through his hair. "It made me feel so helpless. Darci, I can't lock her in her room."

"I know," she said quietly. "I felt pretty helpless, too. I don't know how to keep my son safe if he can't even go to a birthday party without someone threatening to shoot him!" Suddenly, tears sprang to her eyes. "I moved here to give us a fresh start, but it's like we can't get away from Chris's past no matter what we do. Those kids are picking on him not just because of what Mac and Jenny might have said, or what anyone might have posted on the Internet. They're picking on him because of who he is—the kid from Northglenn with the gun."

Jordan set his wineglass down and slipped his arm around Darci's shoulders. "It's going to be all right," he said.

"How?" she asked. "How is Christopher supposed to escape his past when no one will let him?"

"I know what you mean," Jordan said. "I can't seem to get past what happened to Sandra and

Mac." He swallowed hard. "I feel so guilty that there was nothing I could do to stop it. And it wouldn't have happened if it weren't for Sandra trying to please me."

"What did happen?" Darci asked quietly. "Do you feel like talking about it?"

He stared vacantly at the far wall. "It was December 24," he said. "I was minutes away from the end of my shift at the hospital, looking forward to Christmas Eve with my girls, when the ambulance brought them in." Never, if he lived to be a hundred, would Jordan forget the icy fear that had gripped him when his colleague took him aside. "Dr. Samuels had taken the call from the paramedics, who'd followed normal procedure, phoning ahead with details of the victims' injuries." He reached for the wine-glass again, twirling the stem round in his hand. "Normally, names aren't given, only the status and condition of the patients. Details like age, sex and what type of emergency the medics are dealing with.

"But the ambulance driver and paramedics knew Sandra and Michaela. They knew that my world was about to be torn apart. And when Dr. Samuels told me, I just stared at him for a long moment that I'll never forget." He looked at Darci. "His words were like a hatchet to my heart. *The shooting victims are your wife and daughter. My* wife and daughter, not someone else's.

"For the first time in my life, I felt the helpless terror I'd seen so many times in the eyes of my patients' family members. I literally came close to passing out." The intensity of emotion that had gripped him was indescribable. He recalled little about those next few moments. Little except the denial.

Until he'd seen those glass doors open.

"And even though hospital protocol didn't allow me to treat family members, there was nothing I could've done to help Sandra." *Nothing.* Dr. Samuels and the medical team had gone beyond the call of duty in their efforts.

"Later, the television news flashed images of two high school punks in handcuffs—they were the ones who shot up the convenience store. Mac and Sandra had gone there to pick up a last-minute item for our holiday dinner. And do you know what that was?"

"What?" Darci asked, blinking back tears.

"Pecans. For the pie Sandra wanted to make me. It's my favorite, or at least it was. I haven't been able to eat it since." He turned to face her. "It was my fault. If she hadn't gone to the store for the pecans…"

Darci cupped both hands over her mouth.

"Oh, Jordan. It wasn't your fault. It was just a horrible thing that happened."

He felt his eyes mist, but went on. "Sandra was pronounced dead shortly after arrival at the hospital. And I spent the rest of the night sitting at my daughter's bedside, praying like I've never prayed before. She'd taken one .22 caliber bullet to her hip. A second one grazed her face and a third hit her in the chest, missing her heart and other vital organs by inches…a miracle."

He wiped the corner of his eye and faced her. "And now tonight. What's next, Darci?" He took a drink of wine, then set the glass back on the table. "I couldn't fix it. There was nothing I could do to fix it then, and I feel the same way now. I can't stop another punk out there from wanting to go after my daughter."

"They weren't after your daughter," Darci quietly reminded him. "They were after my son. Even though I don't know how you must feel losing Sandra and almost losing Mac, I can at least imagine it. You're not the only one who can't outrun his past, Jordan. I feel like Chris is being made to pay for his crime in Northglenn over and over. And there's nothing I can do about it, Jordan. Nothing—just like you said. All we can do is have faith. Something's got to change."

He reached with one hand to massage the back

of Darci's neck. His caress was gentle, caring. "Lord knows I'm trying to keep the faith," he said. "I just thank God the kids are both safe. I don't want to think about what might've happened. My God, Darci, I've been so selfish. Sitting here pouring out my heart when you must have been just as terrified as I was." He pulled her close. "Come here."

She slid over next to him, and Jordan planted a kiss on top of her head, then simply held her. "I'm truly glad Christopher didn't get hurt."

"Thank you," she said.

"I'd better get home now." Jordan gave her a warm hug then released her. "I promised Mac I'd take her out on the boat tomorrow if the weather's not too nasty. Thank you for listening."

"No problem. It'll be okay, Jordan. Somehow. You'll see."

He nodded. "Good night, Darci."

"Good night."

She shut the door behind him, then turned out the light and went back to bed.

JORDAN THANKED LOUISE when he got home, then went to Mac's room to check on her. She was sleeping soundly, bunched up underneath the covers with her knees tucked up to her stomach. It was as if even in her sleep she was defensive, curled in a tight knot. But at least she was sleeping.

Once in his room, Jordan lay in bed on his back, staring out the window above the bed. He could make out the stars sprinkling the sky. Even though he'd had the glass of wine, he still didn't feel drowsy. What he felt was regret.

After talking to Darci tonight, he knew he couldn't get involved with her. What had happened had shown him—again—that life was both precious and precarious. He could have lost Michaela. Darci could have lost Christopher. Jordan couldn't open himself up to caring about her when there was always the risk, lurking just around the corner, that he could lose her.

Tonight had shaken him up completely. He couldn't let himself get close to Darci and her son. He'd seen so many horrible things in the emergency room. Domestic violence, stabbing victims, parents losing children. So many people suffering. He'd suffered enough, losing Sandra.

He could see Darci socially, but that's where it had to end. He couldn't risk loving her.

And maybe losing again.

DARCI SAT ACROSS THE table from her aunt after telling her what had happened the night before. Stella had gone to bed without watching the news.

"Lord have mercy." Stella clutched one hand to her heart. "Are you sure you feel like being here today? You don't have to give lessons if you're not up to it. I can cover for you."

Darci shook her head. "Nina's riding today, isn't she? I want to talk to her about Christopher." Chris was currently out on a ride with Uncle Leon, who'd thought it best to keep his mind off what had happened the night before and focused on something fun.

"You want to take her lesson?" Stella asked. "We can trade. I'll take Cindy Swanson for you."

"Thanks, Aunt Stella. As long as that's okay with Nina and Cindy, it works for me."

"I don't think they'll mind. It's not the first time you and I have switched."

Nina arrived a half hour later for her lesson, and Darci walked out to her car to talk to her.

"Hi," Nina said, smiling. "You doing okay, Darci? Jordan told me about what happened last night, and I saw the news."

"I'm still a little shook up," Darci said. "When I stop to think what might've happened…"

"But it didn't," Nina said. "And that's the important thing to remember."

"You mind having me for a riding instructor

today?" Darci asked. "I wanted to talk to you, if that's all right with you."

"Of course. That's perfectly fine. What's on your mind?"

"Let's get tacked up first. Ride a little. Then we can talk." With Nina's help, Darci saddled Dollar and Feather and the two women rode the horses to the arena.

Darci demonstrated a few riding exercises for Nina, going over some cavalletti. When they took a break to give the horses a breather, Darci led Nina over to sit on the arena fence.

"You sure you're all right?" Nina asked. "You must have been scared out of your mind."

"I was, that's for sure," Darci said. "But what I'm really worried about is Christopher. Do you think you could fit him in for an appointment sometime in the next couple of days?"

"Of course. Call my office and I'll make sure my receptionist knows to work him in."

"Thank you. I appreciate that. I'm worried about him, Nina. He's pretty shaken. He now knows what it's like when the gun's pointed at you. I mean, he scared all those kids in North-glenn pretty badly, even if the gun he had wasn't real. But he got an even worse shock yesterday when those boys actually fired a real gun at him. I think it's affected him more than he wants to admit."

"I'll talk to him," Nina said. "We'll get it figured out." She paused. "So what's going on with you and my brother?" She gave Darci a crooked smile.

Darci felt herself blush. "We're friends," she said.

Nina chuckled. "I think it's more than that if my brother's actions are any indication. I think he likes you more than a little, Darci."

Darci shrugged. "I like him, too."

"Well, he's too stubborn to know his own feelings, or at least to admit to them," Nina said. "I can tell you that right now. You're going to have to club him over the head to get him to come out and tell you how he feels."

Darci laughed. "I don't know if I'd go that far."

"Don't let him get away," Nina said with a wink. "He's one of the good guys."

Her words stuck with Darci long after their lesson was over. Feeling restless, she searched out Stella.

"I'm going riding for a while, Aunt Stella. Do you mind keeping an eye on Christopher if he and Uncle Leon get back from their ride?"

"Not a bit. You go on and enjoy yourself."

"Thanks. I just need to clear my head."

Darci took Feather through the arena gate, mounted up and headed down the trail. She rode in the direction of the reservoir. Jordan had said he was going to take Michaela out on the boat today. Would they be at the dock? Darci felt a sudden need to be close to Jordan. To make sure he and Mac were all right. She knew she was still shaken.

At the reservoir, Jordan's boat was moored at the dock, his SUV parked in the lot nearby.

"Hello," Darci called out. "Anybody home?"

For a moment, she thought no one was there, then Jordan appeared from below deck.

"Hey," he said. "What brings you out here? Other than your horse." He grinned, and Darci's heart nearly melted.

"Mind if I come on board?"

"Of course not. Come on." He motioned with one hand, and Darci swung down off Feather's back and tied her to a nearby fence.

She boarded the boat. "Where's Michaela?"

"I let her go to Jenny's." He shook his head. "And believe me, that wasn't easy. But Nina thought it would be good for her. Like I said last night, I just want to hover over her, but then the reasonable side of me knows that's not going to work." They sat in the chairs on deck. "I felt like coming out here for a while. The water's so peaceful, even if it is a little cold out."

Darci tugged at the collar of her jacket. "It

is peaceful," she said. "It's a good place to think."

Jordan propped one booted foot on the railing near his chair. "Speaking of thinking, Darci, I've been doing quite a bit of that since last night."

"Oh?" She didn't like the ominous tone of his voice.

"I can't get involved with you, Darci," he said bluntly. "I just don't have it in me to love and lose again. Last night reminded me of Sandra's shooting all over again." His voice grew husky. "I could've lost Michaela. You could've lost Chris. Why risk another person's heart—or your own—when life is so unpredictable?"

Darci didn't know what to say. "Well, I appreciate you being up front with me." At least he hadn't led her on. A lot of guys would've tried to get what they could from her, namely sex. But not Jordan. A part of her felt sad at the thought. She'd enjoyed making love to him, but more than anything, she was falling for him.

She should've been more careful to guard her heart.

"I'm sorry, Darci. I never meant to hurt you."

"It's okay," she said. "You didn't." *Liar.* "I'm glad you were honest with me."

"I didn't mean to lead you on."

"Jordan, it's all right." She wanted to leave,

but she didn't want him to know that he had hurt her.

"But that doesn't mean I don't want to see you at all," he went on. "I enjoy your company, and if you can deal with dinner and a movie once in a while, then so can I."

Dinner and a movie. "Sure, Jordan, that sounds great."

"Good." He reached out and took her hand. "Want to start with tonight? I think we both could use the distraction."

"That would be fine. Officer Gibson is coming over later this afternoon to talk to Christopher. I'm sure he'll be stopping to see Mac, as well."

Jordan nodded. "He called, but I'd already taken her to Jenny's. He's going to go out to the McAllister ranch at four, and I'm meeting him there. So, you want me to pick you up about six? We can grab a bite to eat and go see whatever you'd like."

"Sounds good. Six it is." Darci rose from her chair. "I guess I'd better get back so I don't miss Chris's appointment with Officer Gibson. I'll see you later, Jordan."

"Okay." He brushed a light kiss across her lips. "See you then."

Darci's mind whirled. Was she crazy to agree to see Jordan on a what? A friendship basis? She didn't know if she could do it. She'd begun to feel a lot more for him than friendship, but if that's all he was willing to offer, well, she'd just have to deal with it.

CHAPTER SIXTEEN

JORDAN PICKED DARCI UP promptly at six o'clock. He felt good driving the short distance to her house, knowing he'd cleared the air with her. Now they could go enjoy each other's company without any unrealistic expectations standing between them.

He took her to a Western-themed steak house on the outskirts of town. One famous for its buffalo steaks. They enjoyed their meal, but Darci was quiet as they ate. Jordan figured she was still feeling upset over what had happened to Michaela and Chris.

"You okay?" he asked.

"Fine." She smiled. "You know, Jordan, I don't really feel like going to a movie."

"We can watch a DVD at my house instead, if you'd like," he said. "Louise is sitting with Mac, so she might join us."

"That would be perfect. Chris is staying at Aunt Stella's, since there's no school tomorrow." It was a teacher work day. "I swear, he practically lives out at the Shadow S. He loves it there so much." She looked wistful. "I wish I could provide him with a ranch and a horse of his own."

"Yeah, Michaela's still working on me." He chuckled. "I'm actually thinking about giving in on the horse. Mac's been enjoying her riding lessons so much."

At first, Michaela had been put off by the kiss she'd witnessed between him and Darci. But she'd come around once she realized nothing was really happening. Jordan had sat her down and explained he and Darci were only friends.

"If you want some help picking one out," Darci said, "just let me know. They usually have some pretty good horses at the auction."

He grinned. "Thanks. I'll likely take you up on that offer."

Opting to skip dessert, the two of them headed back to Jordan's place. "Sundays are two-for-one night at the local video store," Jordan said. "How can you beat that for a cheap date?" He winked and Darci laughed.

"Hey, a good deal's a good deal."

Jordan turned onto the street, headed for the video store, just as an oncoming car ran the stop sign and plowed straight into the Explorer.

"I'M FINE." Jordan waved off the nurse trying to get him to go to one of the exam rooms. He had a cut on the side of his head from the broken glass that had flown through the SUV's interior upon impact. But other than that, he was sure he was okay. At the moment he was concerned about Darci.

He pushed back the curtain to the exam room and walked over to the gurney where she lay. "How is she?" he asked Dr. Samuels.

The older man finished checking Darci's eyes with a pen light. "I think she has a slight concussion, but other than that, she seems to be okay. We'll get some X-rays to be sure."

"I told you I was fine," Darci said. "Can I go home now?"

"Not just yet. I'd like you to spend the night for observation, just to be on the safe side."

"Don't argue with the doctor," Jordan ordered.

Darci groaned in protest. "Oh, all right. If you insist. But someone needs to get me a phone so I can call Aunt Stella."

"That we can do," Samuels said. "Tell the orderly who wheels you down to radiology you need to stop and use one of the phones."

"I'll do that," Darci said. She turned to Jordan. "What exactly happened? The last thing I remember is talking about renting a movie."

"A guy on a cell phone ran a stop sign and hit us," Jordan said. "He ran into your side of the

Explorer. Darci, I'm so sorry. There was nothing I could do to avoid it."

"Don't be sorry," she said. "You're not the one who ran the stop sign."

"I'll make up any medical expenses that your insurance doesn't cover."

"Don't be silly. I'm not your responsibility."

But he felt like she was, and he suddenly wished that she was. If anything had happened to her...if he'd lost her...

Jordan could hardly bear the thought.

One more reason not to get close to her. He'd made the right decision. And he planned to stick by it.

DARCI WAS RELIEVED to go home the next day. Aunt Stella arrived to pick her up at the hospital, and Jordan, who was on shift in the E.R., came up to the second floor to see her before she checked out.

"I owe you a movie," he teased. "I'll come by later tonight and see how you're doing, if that's okay."

"It is, but how are you getting around if your SUV was wrecked?"

"It's in the shop, but I—uh—I've still got Sandra's car."

"Oh." She looked taken aback. "Okay, well, come on by if you want to, though I don't make any promises about what kind of company I'll be. I've got a pounding headache."

"Some Tylenol ought to help relieve that," he said.

"So, take two and call you?" she quipped.

"Exactly. See you later, Darci."

After she checked out Darci climbed into Stella's pickup truck. "I fed Sampson," Stella said. Then her gaze raked Darci. "Lord a mercy, girl, I think I'm gonna have a heart attack between you and Christopher! First him getting shot at, and now this." She shook her head. "You sure you feel up to going home?"

"Aunt Stella, I'm fine. Stop fussing."

"Well, if you're not fine now, you should be later."

"What do you mean?"

Stella raised an eyebrow. "Having a good-looking doctor make a house call to check your noggin?" She rolled her eyes. "Are you sure that's all he's checking?"

"Aunt Stella!"

"Just asking." She chuckled. "Seriously, that's awfully nice of Jordan to come over like that."

"I think he feels responsible, even though the accident wasn't his fault. There really wasn't anything he could've done to stop that guy from hitting us."

Stella pulled up in Darci's driveway and

helped her inside. "Are you sure there's nothing I can do for you?"

"I just need to lie down," Darci said.

"Okay. Well, Leon will bring Christopher home after a while."

"I feel like you've done more than your share of watching him lately," Darci said.

"Don't be silly." Stella waved the thought away. "We love having him." She bussed Darci's cheek and headed for the door. "See you later, hon."

IT WAS AFTER SUPPER WHEN Darci heard a knock at her door. She left Christopher loading the dishwasher and went to answer. Jordan stood on the stoop with Michaela.

"Hi. Are you up for some company?"

"Sure." Darci held the door open. "Hi, Mac."

"Hello."

"How are you feeling?" Jordan asked.

"Better. The Tylenol helped."

"Good. We brought movies." He held up some DVDs. "Something for everyone."

Darci spotted an animated film and at least one comedy.

"Chris," Darci called. "We've got company."

Christopher came into the living room not looking extremely thrilled. But he politely

greeted Jordan and Michaela, then invited Mac
to watch one of the sci-fi robot films in his
room.

"So, comedy or action?" Jordan asked.

"I could use a good laugh," Darci replied. "I'm
surprised Michaela and Christopher are getting
along."

"I had a talk with Mac, and she's really sorry
for what she did to him. I think she wants to
make amends."

"That's good. I know Chris won't hold a
grudge against her. He realizes now what she's
been through."

"Good. Maybe the two of them can be
friends."

Darci put the movie Jordan passed her into the
DVD player. While the previews were playing,
he sat beside her on the couch and took her hand
in his.

"There's something I need to tell you," he
said. "I didn't want to say anything when the
kids could hear."

"What is it? Is something wrong?"

"I hope not. That depends on you."

"What do you mean?"

"I didn't want to bring up anything about
the accident in front of them. But I wanted to
tell you how grateful I am that you're all right,
Darci. You gave me a real scare."

"It wasn't exactly a carnival ride for me, either," she said flippantly.

He slipped his arm around her. "Darci, I was wrong."

"About what?"

"About us. Telling you I couldn't get involved with you. I don't want to push you away anymore. What happened yesterday made me realize that life is always a risk. That a person can't walk around scared all the time."

"I see." Darci pursed her lips together. "Well, Jordan, I'm sorry to tell you, but I don't think you were wrong. You see, I can't get involved with you, either. Chris's dad burned me. He turned his back on us on a whim and left me for someone else."

"Darci, I would never—"

She held up a hand. "It doesn't matter. The bottom line is, Ron broke my trust, and I really don't have it in me to trust another man at this point in my life." She gestured with one hand. "Case in point—first you tell me we need to keep our distance, now you're saying you've changed your mind. What's to keep you from changing it again?"

"I won't."

"I don't know that. Jordan, I really like you. I do. But I think you were right in the first place.

We can date without getting serious. Dinner and a movie, right?"

He sighed. "Dinner and a movie."

"Okay." She smiled. "Want some popcorn?"

HALLOWEEN ARRIVED COLD and snowy. The first snow of the season. Christopher still hadn't quite outgrown trick-or-treating, and he insisted on going out in spite of the weather.

"Come on, Mom. It's gonna be my last year to go out. I'll be fourteen next year."

As if she didn't know. Just then, the door bell rang. Darci answered to find Jordan and Michaela, dressed in costumes. Jordan was an Old West sheriff, complete with cowboy hat, badge and a water pistol. Michaela was dressed as a well-known pop star.

"Hi." Darci held the door wide. "Come on in out of the cold."

"Trick or treat," Jordan said. "We thought we'd stop by. Michaela has something she wants to ask Chris."

Christopher, made up as one of the ghouls from Michael Jackson's "Thriller" video, looked skeptical. "What's that?" he asked.

Michaela shifted uncomfortably. "First I want to say I'm really, really sorry about what I did to you at Shannon's party. I never meant to hurt you, Chris, and I'll never forget what you did for me. You saved me from being shot. You saved me from probably getting killed, and I'll never be able to repay you for that."

Christopher squirmed, and Darci was pretty sure her son was blushing beneath his Halloween makeup. "You don't have to make me out to be a hero," he said. "I just did what anyone else would have."

"Chris, don't be modest," Darci said.

"Mom."

"Okay." Darci held up her hands.

"Anyway," Michaela said, "Kelly Parker is having a party tonight, and she told me to bring whoever I want. I'm bringing Jenny for one, and Jenny feels really, really bad about what Ben did to you. We'd both like you to go to the party with us. Ben won't be there. He's grounded, and his mom and dad are making him work off his punishment at his grandpa's cattle ranch. Ben should be dressed up as a horse's butt this Halloween, if you want my opinion."

Jordan and Darci laughed, and Christopher actually smiled. "Well, when you put it that way. Mom?" He turned to Darci.

"You can go," she said, ignoring the nervous butterflies in her stomach. She knew she couldn't lock him in his room.

"Okay then," Jordan said. "You want to ride

with us to drop off the kids? I thought you and I could do something fun afterward."

Darci shrugged. "Sure. I doubt I'll have many trick-or-treaters in this weather anyway. Chris, take Sampson out before we go."

"Okay. Come on, Mac." Chris waved her forward. "You can see how big he's grown."

The kids left the room, and Jordan frowned at Darci. "Where's your costume?"

"Sorry," she said. "I wasn't planning on going anywhere."

"Well, you could always play Kitty to my Sheriff Dillon."

"You know, I think I can do that. Think the kids will mind waiting a few minutes?"

"They have no choice," he said. "I'll go see how they're faring with Sampson while you get ready."

In her room, Darci found a forest-green bridesmaid dress she'd worn in a friend's wedding a few years ago. At the back of her closet, she found the crinkly slip that went with it. It would serve as a passable petticoat. She took a curling iron to her hair and fluffed it into corkscrew curls, using plenty of hairspray. Then she applied an exaggerated amount of makeup, complete with an eyebrow pencil beauty mark. From her jewelry box, she chose a vintage choker along with some dangly earrings and a couple of rings.

Surveying herself in the mirror, Darci decided she made a decent Miss Kitty. She flounced back down the hallway. "Okay, Matt Dillon. I'm ready."

"Mom." Chris grinned. "You look awesome."

"Beautiful," Michaela added.

Darci curtsied. "Why, thank you, young 'uns."

They walked outside and piled into Jordan's Honda. The Parker family ranch lay four miles outside of town. Snow fell in soft flakes for most of the drive there. Jordan and Darci walked the kids up to the door and sudden apprehension seized Darci. Even though Ben and his buddies weren't going to be there, she couldn't help but wonder about the other kids. Again, she told herself she couldn't lock Christopher in a rubber room.

She and Jordan spent a few minutes visiting with Kelly's parents, and Darci felt more comfortable.

"The kids are in good hands," Susan Parker reassured Darci. "I promise, we'll keep a close eye on them."

Darci took Christopher aside for a moment. From her purse, she took out something she'd been thinking of giving him for Christmas. But after what had happened to him at Shannon's party... She handed him the cell phone, already charged and activated.

"This is an early gift from Santa," she said.

Chris gave her a crooked smile, and his eyes lit up. "Thanks, Mom. I really appreciate it."

"You call me if anything goes wrong," she told him. "I mean it, Chris. Anything."

"I will, don't worry." He slipped the phone into the pocket of his ripped jeans.

Darci thanked Susan, then left with Jordan. "So," he said. "What do you want to do, Miss Kitty?"

"Why, I'd say you could take me to the saloon for a sarsaparilla." She gave him a wink. "No beer or wine for designated drivers or their sidekicks."

"Sounds like a winner," he said. "And it just so happens I know of a place with the coldest, sweetest sarsaparilla in town." Then he sobered. "It's called the Drake house. Would you mind, Darci? I want to be by the phone in case— I mean, I have a cell phone, but the bars are loud, and..."

"Say no more," Darci said. "The Drake house sounds good to me."

And then she realized her mistake.

She was going to be alone with Jordan in a cozy house in the middle of a snowfall.

Trick or treat.

CHAPTER SEVENTEEN

"I'M AFRAID I'M FRESH OUT of sarsaparilla," Jordan said, smiling at Darci. "Is Coke close enough?"

"It'll do, Mr. Dillon," she said in her best imitation of Kitty's voice.

Jordan poured them each a Coke, then sat down with Darci on the couch, taking off his hat and setting it brim up on the coffee table. "I'm glad we've got some time alone," he said. "Darci, I've been thinking about what you said the other day. About not trusting men. Not trusting me, basically. Don't you know I would never hurt you?"

She lowered her gaze. "I sure hope not."

"Come here." He took her in his arms and kissed her, long and deep. "Darci, you mean the world to me. I want you to trust me."

"I'm trying," she said. "Just hold me, Jordan. That's all I ask." For now, it was all she could ask. What she really wanted was to make love to him. To get lost in the warmth of his arms and forget about everything that had happened with Christopher and Michaela.

As if reading her mind, he brushed a hand across her hair, trying not to mess up her curls. "Let me show you, Darci. Let me show you how much I care about you."

He sprinkled kisses across her face, lips and neck, holding her tenderly. Then he took her hand and led her down the hall to his room. The bedroom was everything Darci would have expected of Jordan. Masculine, clean and neat. A roomy bed stood beneath the window, covered with a dark blue comforter. An inviting array of king-size pillows and throw cushions lay piled against the headboard. On the far wall stood a dresser with a framed photo of Michaela and Jordan. In it they were on the boat, proudly holding a stringer of fish between them.

Darci breathed in the pleasant scent that pervaded the room—Jordan's cologne. She would never get tired of that scent. Limes and sweet, cold drinks on the beach. But at the moment, the only thing she wanted to drink in was Jordan himself. Darci knew she was a fool. He could break her heart at any time. But for the moment, she didn't care. She wanted only to lie in his arms and forget about what had happened last week. Forget about all the troubles she and Christopher had faced in the past year.

"Jordan," she said. "Make love to me."

"Why, I fully intend to, Miss Kitty," he said, nuzzling her neck.

Carefully, he removed the forest-green dress, unzipping it, and sliding it down Darci's shoulders and hips. He took off her slip and the black pantyhose she'd put on underneath it. When she stood wearing only her underwear, Jordan peeled back the sheets on the bed. She took off her rings and earrings and laid them on the bedside table, her gaze never leaving Jordan's. He reached to undo the snaps of his Western shirt.

"Let me," Darci said, stilling his hands with a touch.

She stood on tiptoe, lacing her arms around his neck, and kissed him deeply. Then her hands found the front of his shirt, and she undid the snaps, slowly and tantalizingly, one at a time. With each snap she unfastened, Darci bent and kissed Jordan's neck, his chest. He groaned and ran his hands down her back, cupping her buttocks. He pressed her against him, and she could feel the hardness of him beneath his jeans. Knowing how much he wanted her sent a little shiver down her back.

When she'd stripped him of everything except his boxer briefs, Jordan took her by the hand and laid her on the bed. They slid beneath the sheets and he held her. "Darci," he whispered. "You make me feel so good. You make me forget all my worries." He kissed her. "You make me happy."

"You do a pretty good job of that yourself, Marshall," she teased. Then she sobered as Jordan unhooked her bra and tossed it aside. He pulled off the pink, lacy panties she wore and ran his hands along her sides, all the way down her thighs.

"You feel so good," he said. "You're so soft… your skin's so silky smooth." He kissed her breast. "I could gobble up every inch of you."

"Don't let me stop you," she said with a mischievous grin.

Jordan captured her mouth in a possessive kiss, and Darci lost herself in loving him. In letting him love her. She told herself to remember this wasn't anything permanent. As long as she kept that in mind, she should be all right.

Jordan kissed her deeply, his hands roving up and down her body. His mouth tasted her everywhere, moving from her lips, across her neck and down to her breasts. He took one nipple in his mouth and flicked his tongue across it. Darci moaned and ran her fingers through his hair, arching her back. His mouth felt warm and good…so right on her flesh. She loved the way his hands felt on her body, his touch firm yet gentle. Caring hands. Loving hands.

He moved his way back up to her mouth again, and Darci relished his kisses, lacing her tongue around his. He pulled away long enough to put on a condom, then wrapped Darci in his arms, and in one smooth motion slid inside her. He rocked against her in gentle rhythm, and Darci sighed, loving the way their bodies fit together, the way it felt as if the two of them had become one.

She wrapped her legs around Jordan's waist and pulled him as close to her as she could. Moving her hips, she matched his speed and rhythm. Jordan reached down and put his hand between them, stroking the tender nub between Darci's legs until she thought she would come unglued.

He wrapped his arms around her and rolled her over, bringing her to rest on top of him. Darci sat astride him, looking down into his dark eyes. "Jordan," she said. "You make me feel so good. You feel so good inside me."

"I never want to leave," he said, and ground his hips against hers. Darci moved in a slow, sensuous rhythm against him. Bracing her hands against his chest, she moved faster and faster against him, then collapsed on top of him as an orgasm shook her.

Wave after wave of pleasure rocked through her body, leaving her quivering, feeling like melted honey. Jordan rolled her over and drove himself more deeply into her, holding her tight against him. Darci again wrapped her legs around him, moving against him. To her delight, a second wave hit her just as Jordan climaxed. Gasping, she held tight to him, and they moved together, heightening their pleasure.

At last, they lay spent in each other's arms. Jordan kissed the top of Darci's head. "That was fantastic," he said. "I don't ever want you to leave this bed, Miss Kitty."

She chuckled. "I think that might be a little hard to explain to the kids, Marshall."

"Speaking of which," Jordan said. "Maybe it wouldn't hurt to call and check on them."

"Good idea." Reluctantly, Darci slid out of bed and found her clothes. Once she and Jordan were both dressed, they headed back to the living room. Jordan dialed Michaela's cell phone and made sure everything was going smoothly at the party.

"They're fine," he said, closing the phone. "They're getting ready to make caramel apples."

"I'm glad," Darci said, letting out a breath she'd barely been aware of holding. "Mind if I use your bathroom?"

"Of course not. It's that way. Second door on your left."

In the bathroom, Darci opened her purse and touched up her makeup. She carried a small bottle of hairspray with her, and used it to put her curls back into place as best she could.

Jordan tapped on the door. "Mac's got a curling iron if you need it," he said. "Actually, there's one under the sink that was Sandra's."

"Oh. Okay, thanks."

"No problem." Darci reached under the sink and pulled out the curling iron. She felt strange, holding it in her hand. *It was Sandra's.* Just as Jordan was Sandra's. He'd kept it all this time, right under the sink, as if his wife was still here, still a part of his household.

Well, wasn't she? Sandra was Mac's mother, and she'd been Jordan's wife. Why shouldn't her presence still be felt in this house?

Darci put the curling iron back under the sink without using it.

Then she left the room, going back down the hall to a man who could never really be hers.

As he drove Mac to the Shadow S, Jordan thought of nothing but Darci. It had been three days since they'd made love on Halloween and he'd never felt so confused. A part of him wanted to keep his distance from Darci, but a part of him wanted to draw her close and hold her there forever.

She was out in the arena when he and Michaela arrived, just finishing up a lesson. Once the student had left, Jordan joined Darci in the arena. Mac went straight over to Dollar, petting him and feeding him a treat.

"It turned out to be a nice day," Jordan said. After a weekend of cold and snow, Indian summer had returned. The high temperature that day was close to sixty degrees, though a few dark clouds now lay scattered in the distance.

"We'd better take advantage of it while we can," Darci said, "since it won't last long. But we've got an indoor arena, so Michaela will be able to continue her lessons all through the winter if you like."

"I'm sure she'll be happy to know that," Jordan said. "I think I'm going to end up getting her a horse pretty soon. I hear the prices are down this time of year, and who am I to pass up a bargain?"

Darci grinned. "That's right, they are. A lot of people would rather sell a horse than have to feed it all winter when they can't ride it. Like I said, just let me know when you're ready to shop and I'll go with you."

"I will. Mind if I stay to watch Mac's lesson today?"

"Of course not." Darci indicated the arena fence. "Pull up a chair." She grinned, then walked over to the horses and untied Feather. "I'll just be a minute, Michaela. I want to switch out horses and give Soot some practice on the cavalletti. Do you think you're ready for them, too?" She smiled as Mac's face lit up.

"Really? You think I'm ready for cavalletti?"

"We'll just do a few laid out on the ground," Darci said. "No big deal, eh?"

"Cool!"

"Want to go with me to tack up Soot?"

"You bet."

They headed for the barn, and Darci led Feather to the hitching post. There they unsaddled and brushed him, leaving his saddle blanket lying upside down on the hitching post to dry the sweat. Darci got another blanket from the tack shed, then caught Soot and let Michaela help her saddle the black mare.

"How's she been doing for you?" Michaela asked.

"Really well," Darci said. "I like her so much, I'd love to buy her from Aunt Stella and Uncle Leon."

"Would they sell her?" Michaela looked eagerly at her.

"Maybe. But it'll be a little while before I can

afford a horse. Meanwhile, at least I can ride her whenever I want."

"You're lucky there," Mac said. She pulled the cinch tight on the saddle, then stepped back for Darci to check it.

"Good job, kiddo." Darci barely had to tighten the leather. "You're getting good at this."

"Thanks." Mac beamed.

With the mare saddled, they headed back out to the arena. Darci helped Michaela mount Dollar, then she swung herself up onto Soot's back. She demonstrated to Michaela how to ride through the cavallettis, taking the horse in a pattern that included some figure eights as they trotted over the poles laid out on the ground.

When they were done, Mac halted Dollar next to Soot. "Can I ride her for a minute?" she asked Darci. "She's so pretty."

Darci hesitated. But they were in the arena, and Soot had been behaving perfectly. "I don't see why not," she said, swinging down off the mare's back.

Michaela dismounted Dollar and tied him to the fence. Then she came over, an eager smile on her face, and mounted Soot. Darci held the mare's bridle while Mac steadied herself in the saddle.

"You'll have to make it a short ride," she said. "Looks like the clouds are moving in."

Midway through the lesson, clouds had begun to scatter across the sky, threatening rain. Typically fickle weather for this time of year.

"I won't take long," Michaela said. "I just want to try her out." But even as she trotted around the arena, over the cavallettis, it began to sprinkle.

Jordan had momentarily disappeared, and Darci saw him now, ducking out of the car with something tucked under his arm. He returned to the arena, unlatching the gate and coming in as Mac trotted around the perimeter.

As she drew close, Jordan called out to her. "I thought you might need this. Your mother always kept it in the trunk."

With that he popped open a bright pink umbrella before Darci could call out a warning.

Soot took one look at the umbrella and spooked sideways, catching Michaela unaware. But to Darci's surprise, Mac managed to keep her balance in the saddle. And then, to Darci's horror, the mare bolted for the open arena gate.

"Mac, hang on!" Darci called. "Grab the saddle horn!"

Without waiting to see what would happen, Darci rushed to the fence and unhooked Dollar's lead rope from his halter. He still wore his bridle over the top of it, so Darci gathered the reins and swung into the saddle.

She took off after Michaela and Soot. The mare had bolted out the gate and headed down the path toward the trails beyond.

Darci hoped and prayed Michaela would be able to stay on her back.

JORDAN WATCHED, HELPLESS, as Mac shot past him on the black mare. Cursing himself for his stupidity, he collapsed the umbrella and ran helplessly toward her. It only took a few steps to realize his mission was futile. Without a horse, he might as well be running in quicksand.

A moment later, Darci flew past him on Dollar, galloping all out in an effort to catch up with Michaela. Jordan jogged down the path after them, saying a silent prayer. He focused on the trail up ahead and watched as Darci quickly closed the gap between herself and Michaela. And then his nightmare came true.

His daughter slipped sideways in the saddle and fell to the ground.

Jordan picked up speed. "Michaela!" he called out. "Don't move!"

He rushed to her side. "Are you all right, honey? Oh, my God, don't move," he repeated.

Michaela groaned, lying flat on her back. "It's my hip, Dad. My bad one. I think I bruised it pretty good."

"I'm so sorry, sweetie, so sorry," he said, moving his hands over her, checking for broken bones. "I had no idea the horse would spook."

"I know, Dad. It's all right."

"Are you hurt anywhere else?" Darci asked. "Oh, Mac, I feel so bad. I never should've let you ride Soot."

"It's not your fault," Michaela said bravely. "I'm the one who wanted to get on her."

Jordan quickly examined Mac, feeling better when he determined she didn't appear to have any broken bones. Still, he wanted to get her to the hospital. "Come on," he said. "Let's get you out of the rain."

"What about Soot?" she asked.

"Don't worry about her," Darci said. "I'll catch her."

But Aunt Stella had come from the barn in time to see what happened, and she now rode down the trail on Feather. "I'll get her," she said. "Don't worry. You all just get in out of this weather."

Leaning on Jordan, Michaela hobbled toward the barn. Darci walked beside them leading Dollar.

"I'm taking you to the emergency room," Jordan said.

"I'm fine, Dad. Really. I just bruised my hip, that's all."

"Just to be sure," he said.

Stella returned a short time later, leading the black mare. "Soot's been doing so good," she said, coming in the barn behind them. "But I guess she doesn't think much of an umbrella."

"Guess not," Darci said dryly. "I truly am sorry, Jordan, for putting Michaela on her."

"You couldn't have known," he said. "I'm the idiot who opened the umbrella."

"You know what you'd have to do if this was the code of the Old West, don't you, Michaela?" Darci teased.

"Get back in the saddle?"

"You've got it. But," she added hastily, holding up a hand at Jordan's protest, "since you're injured, I'll do it for you."

"I don't think that's a very good idea," Jordan said.

"I can't let Soot think she won," Darci said. "She can't think it's okay to buck Mac off, that she got away with something."

"She's right," Stella said.

Jordan shook his head. "I can see right now it won't do any good to argue with you. Better make sure you're wearing a crash helmet."

"I've got my cowboy hat," Darci said, pulling it down low on her head. She went over to the black mare and took the reins, petting the horse's neck soothingly as she spoke to her in low tones. Then she led Soot to the indoor arena.

Jordan and Michaela followed, along with Stella. Darci moved up beside Soot, and the mare shifted restlessly. She spoke to her again, then put her foot in the stirrup and swung on board. Soot took a few quick steps forward, but Darci pulled her in, making her stand.

She stroked the mare's neck again, praising her, then rode Soot in a walk, then a trot, around the arena. She worked her up to a lope, then switched direction, taking her around the arena a few times both ways before riding her back to the gate and dismounting.

"See?" she smiled. "Nothing to it. We'll have to work on her fear of umbrellas at a later date."

"How about working on my fear of you and my daughter riding spooky horses?" Jordan asked.

"She did fine," Darci reassured him as he watched her unsaddle the black mare and brush her down. Michaela, already feeling better, pitched in and helped Stella take care of Dollar.

"You're bound to be the death of me," Jordan said.

"It's okay, Jordan," Darci said. "You just need to relax."

"I'll remember that the next time you're milking a wild buffalo or something," he shot back. "Or riding a wild bull."

She laughed. "Okay, now you're exaggerating."

"Yeah, but not much." He put his arm around her. "Not much at all, cowgirl."

CHAPTER EIGHTEEN

JORDAN HAD LAIN AWAKE half the night after Michaela's mishap with the black mare, tossing and turning, thinking about everything that had happened between him and Darci lately. He'd thought he couldn't allow himself to love her, because he'd been so afraid of being disloyal to Sandra...so afraid of loving and losing again.

But life was risky, and the time he'd spent with Darci finally made him realize he was more than willing to take those risks. He hadn't recognized just how much he truly did love her until he'd seen her in action yesterday, riding after Michaela on the runaway horse. And again, when she'd come to the emergency room with them, waiting to make sure Mac was okay. And that was when he'd made up his mind. He'd decided that he wanted Darci in his life on a permanent basis, and he was willing to do whatever it took to convince her of that.

He had the day off, and while Michaela was at school, Jordan made a trip to town—to the jewelry store. When he'd made love to Darci the other night, she'd taken off the rings and earrings that were part of her Miss Kitty costume and set them on the beside table. One of the rings had fallen on the floor, and when Jordan found it, he'd placed it on his dresser with every intention of returning it. But it had slipped his mind.

Until now.

DARCI WENT RIDING WITH Chris on Thursday to try to relax. Her mind was full of worries. Jordan had been avoiding her ever since Michaela fell off Soot. She figured he must be mad at her for letting his daughter ride the black mare. He hadn't seemed upset at her that day, but then maybe he just hadn't wanted to show his true feelings in front of his daughter.

All Darci knew was he hadn't said more than two words to her whenever she'd run into him at the hospital, and he hadn't called or come over all week.

So she was more than a little surprised when he showed up on her doorstep after her early shift at the hospital on Friday—his day off—wearing his usual ball cap, jeans and boots. He also wore a jacket to protect him from the November wind.

"Hi," he said. "You busy?"

"No," she said. "Come on in."

"Are you getting ready to go to the Shadow S?"

"Actually, I don't have any lessons today. My student who was scheduled for this afternoon came down with the flu."

"How would you like to come out to the boat with me for a little while?" he asked. "This is about the last time I'm going to go to the boat before I dock it for the winter."

"I suppose I could," Darci said. "Just let me get my coat."

He helped her into her jacket, and the two of them headed off in the Ford Explorer, which Jordan had recently gotten back from the body shop. Though the temperature was a bit chilly, the sun was out.

"I was beginning to think you were mad at me," Darci said. "You've barely talked to me since Mac got thrown off Aunt Stella's horse."

"Not at all," he said. "I've just had a lot of things on my mind."

"Oh? Anything I should know about?"

"All in good time," he said.

He parked the SUV and helped Darci out, taking her by the arm. "Watch your step," he said as they boarded the boat.

Then he started the engine, lifted anchor and guided the boat out into the water. "Where are we going?" Darci asked. "I didn't know you were planning to take me out on the boat. I just thought we were going to sit at the dock."

"Don't worry," he said. "We'll be back in time for the kids, and if we're not, I asked Louise to keep an eye on them."

Darci raised an eyebrow. "On Christopher, too?"

"Chris, too." He grinned. "I planned ahead."

"Planned what?" Darci put her hands on her hips in mock indignation. "Just what are you up to, Dr. Drake?"

"You'll see."

He anchored the boat at their special fishing spot, then cut the engine. Sitting beside Darci on the deck, he looked out over the water. No one else was out on the lake. The sun played across the silvery surface, the afternoon rays giving off a little warmth.

"Isn't it beautiful here?" Darci said. "Look how peaceful it is."

"It isn't as beautiful as you," Jordan said. "Which is why I want you to have this." He slipped his hand into his jacket pocket and pulled out a small jewelry box, loving the look of shocked surprise on Darci's face.

"Jordan?"

"Go ahead. Open it." He gestured at the box. Darci opened it, and Jordan nearly laughed at the expression on her face. He knew she'd half expected a ring, from the shape and size of the box. Instead, she stared down at a pair of sapphire earrings.

"Oh, Jordan. They're beautiful." She took one out and held it up to her ear. "What do you think?"

"I think they suit you perfectly," he said. "They match your eyes, and they'll be perfect to serve as your something blue."

"My something blue?" Her breath caught as he pulled a second box from his pocket.

"Your something blue for our wedding—if you'll have me."

He got down on one knee and flipped open the box to reveal the diamond-and-sapphire ring that lay nestled inside. "Darci, will you do me the honor of becoming my wife?"

She gasped and covered her mouth with both hands, then reached out for the box, hands shaking. "Jordan, you're serious."

"Of course I'm serious," he said. "I love you, Darci. And I've come to realize something. After Sandra's death, I was so busy focusing on what I lost, I forgot to really look at what I have. Not just Michaela, but my career. I'd forgotten how to simply live my life to the fullest, helping people, enjoying life. But all that changed when I met you.

"I've been afraid. I kept wanting to fix everything for everybody, including you and Christopher. But I've come to realize I can't do that. And that I can't be afraid of life—I have to accept it with all its uncertainty." He took her hand in both of his and held it. "I was also afraid to let go of Sandra," he said. "I thought loving you would somehow take away from my memory of her, and the life I shared with her. But now I know that's not true, either.

"So, Darci, will you marry me? Will you be my wife, and share your life with me? Be my partner for the rest of our lives?"

A single tear tracked down Darci's cheek. She bit her lip and smiled. "I love you, too, Jordan, and I would be honored and happy to marry you." She held out her hand, and he slipped the ring on her finger.

"It's a perfect fit," she said. "How did you know my ring size?"

Jordan reached once more into his shirt pocket and pulled out the ring she'd left at his house on Halloween. "Simple, Miss Kitty. I cheated."

CHRIS AND MICHAELA WERE waiting at Jordan's house when Jordan and Darci came back from the reservoir. "Where have you been?" Michaela asked.

"Yeah, what's up?" Chris asked. "Louise

came by earlier and told me I was supposed to wait for you here at Jordan's house, Mom."

Darci smiled at her son, feeling somewhat apprehensive. How would he and Michaela take the news? "We have something to tell you," she said, deciding the only way to find out was to simply come out with it. She held out her left hand. "Jordan and I got engaged."

"Oh, my God!" Michaela shrieked. "The ring's gorgeous." She took hold of Darci's hand for a closer look, then smiled up into her eyes. "Does this mean I get free riding lessons from now on?"

Darci laughed. "I guess it does, since I can hardly charge my stepdaughter. And especially since your dad is probably going to get you your very own horse."

"Awesome!" Michaela jumped in the air and hugged first her dad, then Darci.

"Gee, Mom, a guy's the last to know," Christopher teased. Then he hugged her. "Congratulations, Mom. Jordan." He groaned and gave Mac a mock frown. "Does this mean I have to have Michaela for a sister?"

"I guess it does," Darci said.

"That's okay," he said. "Since I know I'll always be the number one child, right, Jordan?" He grinned and Jordan laughed as Mac protested.

"I think that's a spot you're going to have to share," Jordan said.

"Where are we all going to live?" Mac asked.

"I've given that some thought," Jordan said, slipping his arm around his daughter. "How would you feel about selling the house and buying a place with more acreage? Say, enough for my two number one kids to have their horses?"

"Do you mean it, Dad?" Michaela asked, beaming.

"You bet I do, snicker-doodle. But it's also up to Darci."

Darci hugged Christopher with one arm, Mac with another. She peered into Jordan's eyes, happier than she'd ever been.

"Sounds like a plan to me."

CHAPTER NINETEEN

THE WEDDING TOOK PLACE at the ranch Jordan and Darci had purchased on the first Saturday of May. Spring flowers bloomed everywhere along the river, and the weather was perfect. Especially for the ceremony Darci and Jordan had planned.

The entire wedding party was mounted on horseback, including the minister, who preached cowboy church at the local rodeos. Jordan had asked Leon to be his best man, Dr. Samuels his groomsman.

Stella served as Darci's maid of honor and Nina her bridesmaid. Michaela acted as junior bridesmaid, Christopher as usher and ring bearer. Aunt Stella and Uncle Leon mounted up on the two Appaloosas they'd bought at the auction last fall, while Nina rode her own mare—a recent purchase.

Dr. Samuels rode Feather, and Chris rode Dollar, now his own horse. Michaela had a horse, as well—a palomino gelding Jordan had found for her at the horse auction last Christmas.

Darci rode Soot. The mare had become a trust-worthy saddle mount after lots of training and TLC, and Darci had recently purchased her from her aunt and uncle.

The wedding party mounted up beneath an archway decorated with red roses. Jordan sat on Leon's buckskin gelding, Cinch, waiting for his bride.

The skirt of Darci's old-fashioned white lace wedding dress trailed out behind the saddle, draping over Soot's tail. She trotted between rows of folding chairs down the center of the aisle with Uncle Leon, who was giving her away.

Reverend Collins, dressed in a Western suit, boots and a cowboy hat, smiled out at the crowd of people—neighboring ranchers, riding students, hospital workers—who'd come to the wedding.

"Friends and neighbors," he said, "we are gathered here today to witness the hitching up of Jordan Drake and Darci Taylor. They've come to pledge their love to each other before God and before you all here today. If anyone has any objections to that, let him speak now or forever keep his peace." A chuckle rippled through the crowd as one of the horses snorted loudly. Reverend Collins opened his bible and read a few scriptures, then closed the book.

"Jordan, do you have something you'd like to say to your pretty little lady here?"

Jordan scooted his horse sideways, close enough to Darci's to take her hand. "Darci," he said. "It took me a while to realize just how much I love you. But now that I know you're the only woman for me, I hope you'll do me the honor of sharing my life for whatever time on earth the two of us have. I want to wake up beside you every morning and go to sleep beside you every night. I want to share boat rides and sunsets with you, and maybe even a trail ride now and then, if I can manage not to fall off my horse."

Again, the crowd chuckled. "I promise to love you and care for you always, and I promise to play Matt Dillon to your Kitty for as long as we both shall live."

"Jordan," Darci said. "It took me a while to let my heart trust loving you. But now that I have, I know there's no other man for me. I want to share moonlight rides with you, and sunsets on the water. And I want to go to sleep with you each night and wake up with you every morning for the rest of my life. I promise to love you, and treasure you, and be your Miss Kitty for as long as we both shall live."

"And with those words spoken," Reverend

Collins said, "I now pronounce you hitched. Jordan, you may kiss your beautiful bride."

The crowd let out a collective yee-haw, and Jordan leaned in the saddle to kiss Darci, long and sweet.

Then the two of them turned and rode their horses out into a meadow to join their friends and family in celebrating the best day of their lives.

On the ranch at the river's end.

* * * * *